DATING
DR CARTER

BY
JUDY CAMPBELL

D1740362

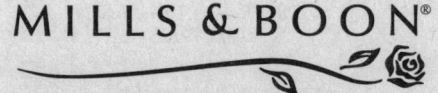

MILLS & BOON®

With love to Helen and Fiona—
with many thanks for their invaluable help.

*First published in Great Britain 2003
Harlequin Mills & Boon Limited,
Eton House, 18-24 Paradise Road, Richmond, Surrey TW9 1SR*

© Judy Campbell 2003

ISBN 0 263 83435 2

*Set in Times Roman 10½ on 12 pt.
03-0303-49113*

*Printed and bound in Spain
by Litografía Rosés, S.A., Barcelona*

'We know each other from somewhere, don't we?'

Iona smiled stiffly, her mouth dry, a ragged flutter in her heart. 'Yes—a few years ago—we did a stint on Orthopaedics at St Olaf's together.'

Matt's grey eyes crinkled and twinkled in recognition. 'God—so we did!' He peered at the badge on her tunic, then laughed delightedly. 'I'm right—it's Iona Bellamy! You've hidden your crowning glory under that cap so I didn't recognise you at first—quite unlike me. Normally I'd never forget a beautiful face—especially as I remember I spent some time trying to get you to go out with me!'

Not lost his touch, thought Iona wryly. OK, so he'd been a flirt, but that hadn't taken away from his sheer likeability—his warmth, humour and kindness.

'It *was* three years ago,' she murmured.

'That long? I'm surprised you remember me…'

Judy Campbell is from Cheshire. As a teenager she spent a great year at high school in Oregon, USA, as an exchange student. She has worked in a variety of jobs, including teaching young children, being a secretary and running a small family business. Her husband comes from a medical family and one of their three grown-up children is a GP. Any spare time—when she's not writing romantic fiction—is spent playing golf, especially in the Highlands of Scotland.

Recent titles by the same author:

THE BACHELOR DOCTOR
TEMPTING DR TEMPLETON
A HUSBAND TO TRUST
JUMPING TO CONCLUSIONS
A FAMILY TO CARE FOR

CHAPTER ONE

THE staff locker room at Sellingford General wasn't the best place to get ready for a glamorous night out, reflected Iona Bellamy. However, despite the difficulties of a shower that spat out spasmodic lukewarm water, and a dimly lit mirror over the washbasins, her friend Chloe Gartside had metamorphosed from a pale-looking registrar in hospital greens to a glossy-looking woman in a sophisticated outfit, and she looked pretty good.

Iona smiled wanly to herself. A few months ago it would have been *her* dashing out on a date after a long shift and looking forward to doing something completely different for a few hours after mending broken bodies in Sellingford's A and E Department. Now, she thought ruefully, work was a way of concentrating her mind on something other than her non-existent social life!

She looked mock-severely over Chloe's shoulder in the mirror as she pulled up the back zip of the little black lace dress for her friend. 'I hope you don't catch pneumonia in this outfit—I hadn't realised it doesn't cover very much! And you'd better not inhale too deeply or this zip won't hold!'

Chloe frowned at her reflection. 'You trying to tell me I'm too fat for this dress?' she demanded, then made a face. 'I should have known better than to borrow something from you, Iona Bellamy—you're a size smaller than I am at least!' She grinned and added with more spirit, 'Anyway, I don't want to look too prudish on my first date…'

Iona chuckled. 'No fear of that, sweetheart—as long as this guy isn't easily shockable!'

Chloe applied lipstick lavishly and then a spray of perfume. 'There—that'll have to do! I wish they'd spend more money on facilities for staff here, never mind the patients!' Then she turned with a smile to Iona and held her hands for a moment. 'You are a star, Iona—thanks a ton for swapping shifts with me tonight and for loaning me the dress. I owe you one! Next time you have a hot date, I'll do the same for you!'

Iona started to pull on her hospital greens, and smiled ruefully. 'Next time I have a hot date could be a few years away,' she remarked. 'You forget— I'm off men for ever and ever!'

'Oh, yeah? I've heard that one before… You wait—I reckon the next handsome guy that comes along will sweep you off your feet. You're ready for some passion!'

'We're not all man-mad, you know!' growled Iona. 'Anyway, I've caused enough mayhem with my attempts at romance—one mistake too many, I think.'

Chloe looked perceptively at her friend for a second and touched her arm. 'Don't be silly,' she said gently. 'You know you did the right thing. One day you'll meet the right man—I'm sure of it.' Then, blowing a kiss at Iona, she tottered out of the locker room on impossibly high-heeled shoes. 'So long, darling. Have a lovely night looking after Sellingford's emergencies—I'll be thinking of you!'

Iona smiled wistfully after her. Chloe might be sure that she'd meet Mr Right eventually, but Iona couldn't be that optimistic, and at the moment Chloe's social life was as hectic as hers was buried under dust! Iona pushed her hair inside the white surgical cap and sighed. Since she and Kevin had split up, the last thing she wanted to do was to have a relationship with anybody else. She'd hurt him badly—and how could she be sure that she wouldn't plunge into another disastrous romance?

She gave a philosophical shrug, and made her way down the corridor to Reception. So—her life was dull at the moment, but better that than the roller-coaster ride of emotions she'd had over the past few months. She didn't envy Chloe her constant dates—not at all! Anyway, she reflected stoutly, working as a registrar in a busy casualty and trauma department, there was no time to dwell on the past.

The waiting room seemed to be filling up. Iona flicked a glance round the room. It looked reasonably quiet at the moment for a Saturday night intake, but from long experience she knew that the whole situation could change in the twinkling of an eye. She sighed as she noticed that already a knot of youths in a corner were laughing in raucous tones as they watched a flickering cartoon on the huge television set on the wall. It wouldn't take much to change the laughter to sounds of abuse if they were kept waiting or someone riled them. More and more it seemed that aggression had become a part of A and E, and that the doctors and nurses were in the first line of attack.

A woman, trying to quieten a screaming baby whilst her young toddler ran round and round the chairs, looked at the youths uneasily, and an old man, shabbily dressed, dozed in his seat, oblivious to the noise going on around him.

'Evening, Jan,' Iona said to Jan Fielding, the plump little staff nurse on night duty, who was wiping the whiteboard clean. Iona jerked her head back towards the waiting room. 'Getting a few customers, I see! Don't like the look of our young friends much.'

'Getting busier by the minute,' replied Jan gloomily. 'You've switched shifts with Chloe, then? I didn't think she'd get anyone to do a Saturday night!'

Iona grinned. 'You know me and Saturday nights! I usually spend them hugging a cup of cocoa and watching telly. Sometimes the excitement's too much and I need to come here for a bit of peace!'

Jan grimaced. 'In your dreams! There won't be time for cocoa tonight. I hate to tell you, but we're down a porter and a staff nurse…*and* a new man started last night to cover for Bernard Smith while he's doing research. Imagine starting a new job at the weekend in Sellingford—it'll certainly test him!'

Iona looked at her in dismay and groaned. 'Oh, no, not more people off ill! I have a gut feeling I'm going to be in a foul mood tonight—is there a flu epidemic or something? And how will we manage without Bernard? He's a terrific registrar. Most selfish of him to do this research.' She sighed, then tried to sound more upbeat. 'Anyway, you never know—this guy may be just as good. Do we know anything about him?'

Jan brightened up slightly and grinned. 'It was like a madhouse last night, so I didn't see much of him— just enough to know that he'd raise any girl's blood pressure! Drop-dead gorgeous and just back from doing everything you can imagine in the wilds of Mozambique on some charity project. I guess there's not much he can't do—although,' she added pessimistically, 'he may find he wishes he was back in Africa and not coping with the chaos here in A and E.!'

'You don't know that!' said Iona brightly, 'He could be just the person!' She looked at the handover notes from the last shift. 'What's going on in the majors area?'

'An elderly lady with a suspected myocardial infarction and a man with multiple fractures from an RTA. He's been X-rayed, and we're monitoring the heart patient. Bet Lucas, Sister on duty, is with her now.'

'And who's with the fracture patient?'

'Piers Conlan is assessing him. Apparently one of his legs is in a bad way and he's got to be stabilised before he goes up to Orthopaedics.'

Iona nodded, relieved that the casualty consultant, Piers Conlan, was there. He was a specialist in trauma injuries, from fractures to head wounds, and, although relaxed in most situations, would not tolerate sloppiness in his department.

She checked her watch. 'Right—I'll go over there in a minute. Time for us to do a bit of hands-on now. Would you go with Lucy and see the little boy in cubicle two with a bad cut and graze? She ought to get a bit of experience cleaning and dressing. I'll go and see if I can find our new registrar and then go and check on the majors.'

She walked briskly off down the corridor, already into the swing of the night shift. The noise in the waiting room seemed to be getting louder—in fact, it was beginning to sound like a lot of nights in Casualty, reflected Iona wryly. She frowned and walked more quickly towards the area, taking a deep breath as she saw one of the youths who'd been waiting earlier shouting at Connie, the receptionist. He was hitting the desk with one hand and shaking a fist at her with the other, leaning over so that his face was a few inches from the glass panel that protected her from the general public.

'What the hell d'you think yer doing, keeping us waiting like this? My mate's ill—he's been vomiting. You get us seen to now or, I'm telling you, I'll give you something you won't forget in a hurry.'

Connie, a sweet-natured girl from the West Indies, stared unblinkingly back at him—it was a scenario she was only too familiar with. 'Sorry, sir,' she said with just the slightest inflexion on the 'sir', 'but he'll have to wait his turn…'

'We'll be complaining to the authorities. Call yourself an emergency unit. It's a joke!' He gazed menacingly round the room at the apprehensive patients staring at him. 'And what are you lot looking at? Seen something funny, have you?'

'Excuse me, is there something wrong?' Iona's voice cut in loudly and calmly over the lout's aggressive tones. Her experience over the years in A and E departments had taught her that the cooler one sounded the lower the emotional temperature stayed.

The youth whipped round and looked her up and down insolently. 'I'm telling you, lady, we need to be seen now or we'll sue for…for negligence! You in charge of this dump?'

'I'm a registrar on this unit. Your friend's been seen by the triage nurse, but at the moment we have some more urgent cases than his. He'll be seen very soon.'

'Yeah? We've heard that before.' He stepped towards her and thrust his face forward, wagging an aggressive finger at her. 'Listen, you loser, get me mate seen to, or else…'

Iona clenched her hands in her pockets and wished, not for the first time, that she was an eighteen-stone, six-foot-four man—at a petite five feet five inches she didn't present much of a threat to this yob. She tried not to flinch as his other hand bunched up in a fist, tensing herself for the blow she was sure he'd land on her chin.

The large figure in a white coat that suddenly stepped in front of her made her blink in surprise, interposing itself between her and the youth and shooting out a large hand that held the boy's fist in a vice-like grip.

'Have you got a problem?' The deep voice was pleasant but dangerously quiet, and the newcomer stood a good six inches taller than the youth. 'Perhaps you'd like to explain what's going on?'

He gripped the youth's wrist tighter so that it whitened, and the boy yelped. 'You're hurting me… Stop it!'

The man chuckled as he dropped the youth's hand. 'Not such a big man after all, are you? Come on, sunny boy, tell me what you have in mind.'

A look of startled apprehension crossed the young oaf's face. 'We shouldn't have to wait this long,' he muttered sullenly. 'Anyway,' he added with sudden spirit, 'who the hell do you think you are?'

The man smiled, but it didn't reach his eyes. 'I'm a specialist registrar on this unit—ultimately I make the decisions about what order patients are seen. Patients are dealt with according to the gravity of their

situation. And by the way, I don't like the noise you
and your mates are making—this is a hospital, not the
local pub. The man who's waiting to be seen can
stay—the rest, out!'

'What? You telling me we've got to go?'

'Got it in one.' The man's voice was pleasant.
'Glad you've got the gist of it—goodnight!'

The yob glared aggressively up at him, and the man
held his gaze with hard grey eyes. Sullenly the youth
looked away then sloped back towards his mates,
kicking chairs as he went.

'Come on,' he growled to his companions. 'Let's
get out of this dump. They're a bunch of gits in here!'

Everyone's eyes in the waiting room followed the
surly crowd of youths as they made their way out,
shouting obscenities to each other. Iona heaved a sigh
of relief as the tension in the room dropped immediately—a bunch of yobbos like that frightened
everyone.

She looked at Connie who was staring at the scene
with an open mouth. 'You OK?' she asked.

Connie shrugged and grinned. 'I am now, aren't I?
After the arrival of Superman here—what a relief!
What planet does he come from?' she asked in a stage
whisper. 'He can't be for real, a hunk like that! He
must be the guy who started last night when I wasn't
on.'

She turned to answer the phone, and for the first
time Iona looked directly at the man, now standing
with his arms akimbo, watching the departing trou-
blemakers with narrowed eyes. She blinked for a second, wondering if her eyes were deceiving her, then
a sudden little shiver zipped through her body and
made the hairs on the nape of her neck stand on end.

The past few minutes had been so tense she hadn't really concentrated on anything except the scene going on in front of her. Now, staring at the tall man a few yards away, it hardly seemed possible, but there was something very familiar about that short dark hair, deep voice and formidable physique. She gazed at him incredulously, then drew a deep breath and licked her dry lips.

'Thanks for coming to the rescue there,' she said a little croakily. 'Things might have got out of hand—Security isn't always very quick.'

The man turned to smile at her, his grey eyes warm and twinkling. 'Glad to be of help. Didn't want to break up the party between you and that young charmer, but I couldn't resist it!'

Iona smiled bleakly to herself. Of course he wouldn't remember her. In the mad jumble of a busy orthopaedics ward, Matthew Carter and she had worked together for six months—and they'd had one date! He didn't know it, but because of him she'd nearly made the biggest mistake of her life.

She jerked back to the present as the man held out his hand. 'Can I introduce myself? Matthew Carter, filling in for Bernard Smith.'

He hesitated for a moment as he looked at Iona, then frowned, tipping his head on one side. 'We know each other from somewhere, don't we?'

Iona smiled stiffly, her mouth dry, a ragged flutter in her heart. 'Yes, a few years ago, we did a stint on Orthopaedics at St Olaf's together.'

The grey eyes crinkled and twinkled in recognition. 'Yes—so we did!' He peered at the badge on her tunic, then laughed delightedly. 'I'm right—it's Iona Bellamy! You've hidden your crowning glory under that cap so I didn't recognise you at first. Quite unlike me. Normally I'd never forget a beautiful face—especially as I remember I spent some time trying to get you to go out with me!'

Not lost his touch, thought Iona wryly. Still coming out with the old familiar chat-up lines, ready to flirt with anyone who had a pulse and was female! She softened slightly. OK, so he'd been a flirt, but that hadn't taken away from his sheer likability—his warmth, humour and kindness, not just to patients but to anyone feeling a little low.

'It *was* three years ago,' she murmured.

'That long? I'm surprised you remembered me.'

Iona suppressed the desire to retort that she never forgot a handsome guy, but seeing him standing before her with the same smile, the same warm grey eyes, was like being in a time machine, bringing the old feelings back vividly, a bitter-sweet memory when every day on orthopaedics had been enlivened by working with him. He had been the love of every girl's life on the unit then—and had had a reputation to go with it. That was why, however much she'd yearned for him, Iona had kept herself in the background. She hadn't wanted to end up as one of his romantic casualties—friendship was all she'd hoped for.

Matt leant forward and held both her shoulders, looking down smilingly at her face. 'This is great!' he enthused. 'We'll be working together again! I remember we had a lot of fun before...'

'Yes, we did...a lot of fun,' murmured Iona hollowly, the touch of his hands sending shock waves through her body. She stepped firmly away from him for a moment, regaining her composure. She sure wasn't going to be soft-soaped into falling for his charm again. She'd learned her lesson—hadn't she?

Matt hadn't been the type to be serious—life had been for enjoyment and for living well. He had flitted from one girl to another like a bee in search of honey. Why, then, when she'd known what he was like, had she been such a fool as to accept his invitation to a summer ball held in a nearby stately home at the end of their six-month rotation? She'd told herself that it was just a casual date—after all, a girl didn't fall hook, line and sinker for someone after just a few hours!

Now that magical evening came back to her as clearly as yesterday. Iona knew there had been something special between them—a magnetic attraction that had been more than physical. When the dance had come to an end she had been sure it would be the start of something wonderful. How wrong she'd been! The time on Orthopaedics had drawn to a close and they'd gone their separate ways. She'd never heard from him again—and the consequences for herself had very nearly been disastrous.

Iona looked at Matt more coolly, irritated with herself for reacting like a teenager confronted with a pop star. Perhaps, she reasoned, it was the total shock of seeing the man again—a kind of reflex action of how she used to feel when she worked with him three years ago. And that was just it, she said sternly to herself, he was an attractive man whom she'd once dated in the past, and a lot had happened to her since then. Now he was nothing to her. There should be no reason on this earth for her heart to thud against her ribs, or for her mouth to dry up…

His warm voice cut into her thoughts again. 'I look

forward to you showing me round the place—last night there wasn't time to breathe.'

'I'm not normally on this shift,' Iona countered firmly, trying to maintain a distance between them.

Matt flicked a quick glance at her, as if he'd caught her tone. 'Then we'll have to try and do everything tonight,' he said with a smile.

Iona looked at him under her lashes. He looked just as devastating as he always had, except that his face was tanned more than you'd expect from the summer weather in Sellingford, and his springy dark hair was shorter. Probably the one thing that hadn't changed, she thought darkly, was his reputation for playing the field where girls were concerned!

Matt had started flicking through the files of the patients' notes that had already been written up. He looked up quizzically at Iona. 'Looks as if we'll have a busy night—but you and I have some catching up to do when we have a quiet moment,' he said breezily. 'I want to hear about *everything* that's happened to you since we last worked together. Where you live, where you've been working—your love life…'

Those clear grey eyes laughed down at her and, despite herself, Iona again felt the treacherous thrill of attraction run through her like an electric shock. It was ridiculous, but it frightened her. It had been too long since she'd felt like this—the sudden weakness in her knees, the fluttering of her heart against her ribs. Disturbingly, Matthew Carter seemed to have awakened parts of her she'd thought had sunk into irreversible coma!

She swallowed and said coolly, 'I'm afraid there won't be much to tell. And now I'd better go and—'

The sudden sound of the cardiac alarm squealed

down the corridor and drowned the rest of her words. Matt's eyes met hers with humorous exasperation.

'Wouldn't you know it? These patients have no consideration…'

Then with one accord both doctors sped off towards the majors area and into the resus unit, almost crashing into Jan and the student nurse, Lucy Brogan, as they appeared from another direction.

Iona felt the familiar rush of adrenalin as she responded to the emergency, and with the ease of practice slid into the co-ordinated group of people that made up a crash team.

Gladys Keane was the patient who'd been brought in earlier after a suspected heart attack. She looked a tiny, rather pathetic figure lying spotlighted on the bed, myriad tubes and flashing lights of monitors surrounding her. Sister Bet Lucas was inserting a plastic airway into the woman's mouth. Matt slid round to the side of the patient, hooking his stethoscope into his ears and putting the trumpet end on Mrs Keane's chest.

'Patient started choking, turned blue…tachycardic,' said Bet. 'Looks like she's having an acute MI.'

'Right,' said Matt brusquely, still listening intently to the woman's chest. 'Start by giving her some strong mouth-to-mouth…and we need bloods and drugs.'

Smoothly the team went into practised action, and although on the surface the activity seemed frantic and slightly manic, underneath there was a sense of calm co-ordination. Speed was essential in the first stages of acute cardiac failure. Bet pinched the patient's nostrils together and started to blow sharply down the airway, her eyes flicking to Mrs Keane's chest to see if the lungs were inflating. Jan quickly unrolled a pack of pre-packed injectible drugs from the resuscitation trolley and Iona searched for a vein to draw off blood from the patient's thin arm.

Matt looked up, his voice sharp. 'We'll have to shock her,' he said tersely, still listening intently to his patient's chest. 'She's got ventricular fibrillation…nothing happening…'

Jan Fielding unhooked the paddles from the defibrillation machine and handed them to Iona, who placed one under the heart and one on the upper right of the chest as Matt moved away.

'Charging the defibrillator now—200 joules,' she said. 'Stand back, everyone…'

Mrs Keane's frail body arched off the bed as the current surged through her chest, and Matt put his stethoscope on her chest and listened to her heart.

'Give her another one,' he said tersely.

Iona repeated the exercise. 'Another 200 joules—stand back now.'

This time Matt's face changed to a look of relief. 'Got it!' he said. 'We've done it—she's back again!'

Iona flicked a glance at the oximeter by the bed, which gave a continuous reading of Mrs Keane's blood pressure and oxygen levels.

'BP 80 over 50, sats 85…heartbeat 110,' she read out. 'Has she had streptokinase?'

'Yes, on admittance,' said Jan. 'She looked like she could have a blockage. She had 300 milligrams aspirin in the ambulance and door to needle time was only ten minutes.'

'I think she's settling back into sinus rhythm,' said Matt, his eyes fixed on the trace, still listening intently to her heart. 'The beat's more regular.'

There were a few seconds of tense silence as the team watched the electrocardiograph trace, then finally Matt stood up from his bent position over Mrs Keane's body and nodded.

'Think we've been lucky this time—managed to avoid a complete arrest. We need to get her down to CCU pronto. Give her some oxygen and check the blood gases—she may need some intravenous sodium bicarbonate to correct acidity in the blood.'

Jan fitted a mask over Mrs Keane's face and a porter immediately took her down to the cardiac care unit.

Matt blew out his cheeks in relief and smiled round at the team. 'Thanks, everyone. That was a narrow squeak. I'd better have a word with the consultant now.'

'Mr. Harman's on his way down,' said Bet.

There was a general lessening of tension and the atmosphere eased. Iona glanced round at the disparate group of people who had made up the team trying to pull Mrs Keane through the emergency and smiled to herself. This was the good side of Casualty—saving someone out of the split-second drama that happened in this department as in no other. Here there was no predictable pattern of recovery—unlike a ward, you took whatever random illness or injury was thrown at you, and whether you were familiar with the problem or not, did your best. And that was part of the excitement, thinking on your feet!

She looked across at Matt and reflected how well he'd fitted into the team although he'd only just joined the unit—efficient, low-key and calm.

Ten out of ten so far for medical technique, Dr Carter, she admitted to herself.

In the tense minutes they'd been treating the emergency she'd put Matt out of her mind, but now that they'd relaxed and he was standing just a few feet away from her, he surged back into her awareness. As if conscious of her scrutiny, he looked up and met her eyes.

'A good ending,' he said with a buoyant grin. 'Makes you feel great, doesn't it?'

His enthusiasm was infectious and she couldn't help giving him a wide smile in return. 'It sure does,' she answered, before going quickly to the basin and washing her hands.

His eyes followed her for a second as he stuffed his stethoscope into his pocket.

'Don't forget our appointment together,' he murmured. 'What about coffee in half an hour?'

'We'll see,' she said guardedly, part of her wanting to catch up on his past, part of her wary of his power to captivate.

The door opened and Luke Harman came into the room, almost colliding with Matt. A look of pleased surprise crossed his face.

'Good heavens—it's Matt Carter! Fancy seeing you here!' He shot out his hand and shook Matt's vigorously. 'I heard you might be joining us. I think the last time we were together was at a rather drunken leaving party for you at St Olaf's! I thought you'd taken off for somewhere exotic after that—what's brought you back to the bright lights of Sellingford?'

Iona looked up with interest—she had wondered that, too. Why come back to an out-of-the-way place like Sellingford? She'd have thought a man of Matt's energy would have preferred a place more at the cutting edge of medicine. She looked at him curiously.

Was it her imagination, or was there the slightest pause before he answered, a shuttered expression darkening his eyes momentarily? Maybe, she reflected, Matt had a hidden agenda in his reasons for returning to the area.

To her ears his short laugh seemed rather forced, but he said easily enough, 'Life moves on, you know. Felt an urge to come back to my roots and all that. The old place has a certain appeal.'

Luke grinned. 'Well, it's great to see you again— and I expect your father, Professor Carter, is delighted to have his son and heir back in town!'

'I intend to keep out of his way as much as possible.' Matt smiled. 'He's retiring from the hospital soon, so I'll be able to relax more!'

'We'll miss him,' said Luke. 'By the way, I take it you've come as Bernard Smith's replacement?'

'That's right. I think he'll be a hard act to follow, though...' He held the door open for the consultant and they started walking down the corridor. 'Perhaps I could fill you in on Mrs Keane's case as we go up to CCU. As you know, she was brought in with a suspected myocardial infarction, and suddenly went into ventricular fibrillation about twenty minutes later...'

Their voices faded into the distance, and Iona helped Jan push the now redundant equipment back against the wall.

'Wasn't I right?' said Jan, standing with her arms akimbo and looking slightly smug.

Iona looked at her, puzzled. 'About what?'

'Dr Carter, of course. Eat your hearts out, gorgeous doctors of the world—I've found someone else to make my pulses race!'

'I was too busy to notice,' said Iona primly. Then she caught Jan's eye and gave a chuckle. 'I should think he's well aware of his attraction! I hadn't realised that he was Professor Carter's son,' she added thoughtfully. The professor was the grand old man of medicine at the hospital, and hugely respected.

Bet put her head round the door. 'Would you have a word with Mrs Keane's relatives?' she asked. 'I'm afraid the poor things were pushed into the corridor rather brusquely when things got hectic in here... we'd better put them in the picture.'

'Sure, I will,' agreed Iona, glad to turn her mind to something that didn't include Matt Carter.

She slipped out to where a bewildered-looking elderly man and a woman were standing against the wall in the passageway and smiled at them reassuringly.

'Mr Keane? I'm Dr Bellamy, and we've just been looking after your wife. If you come with me to the relatives' room I'll explain what has been happening. I expect you've been very worried.'

The woman stepped forward anxiously, her eyes red and puffy. 'I'm her daughter. We heard the alarm going off and they wouldn't allow us to stay in. Is...is she all right? Where have they taken her to?' Her voice trailed off miserably, and she dabbed a handkerchief to her mouth with a trembling hand.

Gently Iona shepherded them to the more private area set aside for relatives, and they sat down nervously on the edge of their seats, uncomfortable and scared in the alien atmosphere of the hospital.

Iona spoke softly and clearly, knowing that it would be difficult for them to take too much in. They were both in shock, the dramatic events of the past few minutes having throwing them off balance. They needed to be reassured and encouraged to try and talk things through with each other.

'As you know, we were monitoring Mrs Keane very carefully after she was brought in with a suspected heart attack. Suddenly her heart muscle, her left ventricle, began to fibrillate—that is, go out of rhythm—and the blood wasn't able to pump round her body efficiently. Naturally it was very important that we got the heart back to a more stable state. I'm sorry you had to be pushed out of the way—there were a lot of people round her.'

The woman clutched her father's hand. 'Did...did it settle down?'

'Fortunately she was in the right place at the right time and we were able to calm things down and get her heart back into rhythm again. It was a good job she was brought here so quickly when she first felt ill—it's given her every chance. Now she's been taken to the cardiac care unit where she'll be monitored very closely.'

'Will she get better?' quavered the old man. 'We...we've never been apart for fifty years...'

He looked pleadingly at Iona as if she could promise him that things would be the same as they used to be, demanding a positive answer.

Iona touched his arm gently. She could never give guarantees. 'Your wife is still very ill,' she said quietly, 'As I said, however, being here when she had the fibrillation was very lucky, and although she's not out of the woods yet, she has every chance of getting over this. Look,' she said more brightly, 'why don't you and your daughter have a cup of tea? The consultant will be down soon to tell you her progress. I don't know if you'll be able to see her just yet—but try not to worry.'

Mr Keane nodded. 'Thank you, Doctor. We appreciate your time.'

The old man looked more composed, and as she went out of the room Iona reflected that the old well-worn phrases did have their uses—they were familiar and calming words in a frightening situation. Already father and daughter had started to talk things over, trying to adjust to the fact that the woman who'd been the centre of their world, and whom they'd thought indestructible, had been taken ill so suddenly.

Leaning against the wall outside the relatives' room with his hands in his pockets was Matt, a quiff of dark hair standing up on his forehead. He smiled at Iona as she came out.

'All done? Then we've got a five-minute window for you to update me on your life and drink the most delicious hot fresh coffee you can imagine…'

Iona bit her lip, trying to dampen the treacherous somersault her stomach did when she saw him unexpectedly. 'I…I have some paper work to do. It can't wait.' she countered firmly. 'We can catch up another time maybe…'

Another time, she thought, when I'm more used to the idea of working next to Matt Carter again!

Matt laughed, a deep throaty chuckle. 'Come on, now,' he said gently, taking her arm and starting to propel her down the corridor to the kitchen. His eyes looked down at her penetratingly. 'I won't take no for an answer—although I get the distinct impression you're backing off rather hard!'

Iona coloured slightly. 'Don't be silly. It's just that I need—'

'What you need, Iona Bellamy,' he said firmly, 'is an injection of one hundred per cent caffeine with me.'

His eyes twinkled down at her, clear, warm and sexy, and Iona bit her lip. This man's arrogant belief in his own attraction and his confidence hadn't changed at all since she'd last seen him—and she was darned if she was going to be bullied by him into what he wanted her to do. No way, she said sternly to herself, was she going to be under his spell again…

He was very close to her. For a brief moment she allowed herself to dwell on his strong face and mobile mouth, and suddenly it was as if time had stood still since that dance three years ago when she'd felt his animal attraction hit her like a bolt of electricity. She couldn't help herself.

'Very well, just a quick cup,' she sighed, and allowed herself to be steered towards the kitchen.

CHAPTER TWO

IT WAS almost a relief when the casualty consultant, Piers Conlan, stopped them on their way to the kitchen as Iona was beginning to regret that she'd agreed to have coffee with Matt. She didn't feel like having an in-depth discussion about her life since she'd left St Olaf's. Matt may have awakened some memories, but she was trying to forget the past, not bring it up again.

'Something for us, Piers?' she asked, trying to hide the eagerness in her voice.

'Got two lads in the trauma room,' Piers informed them. 'Their friends brought them in. Been having a pleasant night out at a club, it seems—usual way of enjoying themselves, sticking broken bottles in each other's faces.' He shook his head helplessly and sighed. 'I dunno, *I* used to get my kicks doing ballroom dancing on a Saturday night... Anyway, see what you can do with them.'

'We'll put that coffee on hold,' murmured Matt, as they went into the clean trauma room where surgical procedures such as stitching and removing foreign bodies could be performed.

Two large youths lay on two of the beds, each with bloodied faces. One was groaning loudly and assuring the people in the room that he was going to get even with the man who'd done this to him. The other man lay still with his eyes closed and a deep laceration on the tattooed arm flung across his chest.

'I'll take the chatty one,' said Matt, as he and Iona pulled on latex gloves and masks.

He bent over the first man and looked closely at the deep cut to the side of the patient's face, sniffing the man's breath and making a face.

'You've had a few bevvies, haven't you? That's probably why you're bleeding so much. What happened?'

'Someone mouthed off at us. We gave him what he deserved and he came back at us with a bottle... The *bastard*.'

'Ah...I see... Can we have blood from both patients for cross-matching, please? If it looks too bad they may have to go to Surgical later.'

He started to swab the wound to the man's face. 'You're Carl Brown, right?'

'Yeah, and don't you hurt me,' snarled the man.

'I'll be very gentle with you,' Matt assured the patient primly, as he started to clean the wound and get out any fragments of glass. 'You're lucky—this looks worse than it is. I'll be able to suture it OK'

The man grunted. 'Hope you've done this sort of thing before. I don't want a socking great scar on my face...'

Matt grinned. 'Never done it in my life, but don't worry—I won't mar your beauty. You'll look like a pop star when I've finished with you.'

The patient gave an unwilling chuckle, and Iona smiled as she started to examine her patient, Bert Phillips. Matt Carter knew how to keep the atmosphere light. It was a very necessary part of Casualty—not in life-and-death situations, but if aggression could be defused it acted as an escape valve

for the tension and fear that every patient had, even
such a tough nut as Bert Phillips!

She frowned as she started to examine Bert, palpating his abdomen for signs of internal injury, noting
the skin and muscle that had been gouged out of the
wound on his arm. His head laceration seemed su-
perficial but a large purple bump had formed above
his right temple. She opened his eyes and shone her
penlight into them.

'Pupils reactive,' she murmured. 'What's his
Glasgow coma scale, Jan?'

Jan had been trying to clean the patient's arm. 'It
was fifteen when he was brought in,' she replied. She
grimaced as she inspected the wound. 'There's a lot
of torn muscle and ligament here—I don't think we're
going to be able to do much.'

Iona bent down to Bert's ear and said clearly,
'Bert…Bert, how are you feeling?'

'Absolutely awful,' said the man thickly, his voice
slurring. 'Got…got a thumping headache and my
neck hurts.'

'Just dress that arm for now, Jan. You're right, it's
a real mess. He's going to need surgery on it from
the plastics people,' said Iona. 'We'll put a collar on
his neck and X-ray for possible fractures.' She went
across to Matt and said in a low voice, 'I'm concerned
that this man's got signs of neurological deterioration
here—I think he needs a CAT scan. Would you take
a look at him?'

Matt came round to Bert's side and took a pencil
from his pocket, running it along the sole of the man's
foot, which remained flaccid.

'No plantar response,' he said. 'I think you're right,
Iona—there could be an arterial bleed from that blow

to the head. I'll ring to get a slot for a scan if you like.'

'When can we get out of here?' demanded Carl, struggling to sit up. 'I've got to get Bert home soon.'

'Bert's not going anywhere at the moment,' said Iona. 'He's going to be under observation for at least twenty-four hours, if not longer, and his arm will need surgery—and I don't think that will be until tomorrow.'

'What?' The burly Carl heaved himself into a sitting position. 'I don't believe this! You've got to let us out. We're not prisoners.'

'What's the rush?' said Matt, who had come back into the room. 'Your friend's seriously hurt—he's not fit to go home yet.'

Carl stabbed a forceful finger at him. 'I'll tell you what the rush is, mate. Tonight was Bert's stag night—it's his wedding day tomorrow and his bride's going to throw a wobbly when her groom doesn't turn up!'

Matt's eyes met Iona's for a second. 'Well, Mr Brown,' he said smoothly, 'you'll just have to use all your powers of diplomacy to explain to his intended why he'll be unable to get to the church on time!'

Iona held the mug in her hands and inhaled the aroma of hot roasted coffee in the kitchen where she and Matt were sitting.

'I hadn't realized how much I needed that—we must have been a good hour coping with those two men and I'm exhausted!' she declared, leaning back in her chair. 'This tastes about a hundred per cent better than usual—it can't be the instant stuff!'

'That's because I made it,' said Matt modestly. 'I

also happened to grind the coffee freshly before I came in—I can't get through a shift without it. Hopelessly addicted! It's one of my weaknesses!'

That, and playing the field, thought Iona drily.

'Quite a night so far,' Matt remarked. 'I feel rather sorry for Bert's future wife—I should think she's in for a lifetime of watching fights from the sidelines.'

They both chuckled, recalling Carl Brown's indignant face when told he couldn't take his mate home. After the tension of the last hour, it was good to unwind for a few minutes and recharge their batteries. Iona relaxed back in her chair and sipped her coffee gratefully, putting her feet up on a little stool in front of her.

There was a short silence, then Matt leant forward, his glance sweeping over her keenly. 'You haven't changed at all,' he said in a low voice. 'You look marvellous! I can't believe it's three years ago since we last met...'

She laughed. 'You're asking me to believe that— pull the other one! I know what I look like in this outfit—and it's certainly not marvellous!'

'I never say anything I don't mean, Iona,' Matt protested. He took a swallow of coffee, looking at her over the rim of his cup. 'Don't put yourself down.'

She glanced away, telling herself that Matt couldn't help delivering these chat-up lines, albeit with charm and a kindly humour. Neither could he help it that every single thing about him screamed of sexual attraction, from the long legs stretched out in front of him to the lean, taut body propped up on the chair. Her eyes rested for a second on his short, rather spiky dark hair and his strong mobile face. Seeing him again, hearing his voice, awoke a mixture of emotions she hadn't felt for a long time, and a vague feeling of panic fluttered through her—she wasn't ready for a heart to heart just yet, and Matt was watching her with his bright, clear eyes as if waiting for her to start on her life history.

All at once the room seemed rather small for the two of them, the atmosphere a little too cosy. Far from getting used to Matt's heady presence, she seemed to be increasingly aware of him, even when he said something totally crass—probably the kind of thing he said to all the girls.

She cleared her throat and said quickly, 'We mustn't stay long. Piers is a bit of a stickler for keeping on top of things, and there's been some more admissions...'

Matt smiled wryly. 'Work comes first, I know!' He got up and leant against a cupboard, looking down at her, his eyes twinkling. 'Looks like we'll have to have another session after work, then, some time—we have some serious catching up to do. I seem to remember you had a very active social life and the only time I could get a date with you was the week before we finished our orthopaedics stint.'

And with good reason, thought Iona. I didn't want to be one of the many you abandoned after whirlwind romances. And then, of course, I caved in—went out with you and fell head over heels in love with you in one night!

Then a smile twitched her mouth momentarily. '*I* had an active social life? What about you? Sometimes we were surprised you managed to fit work in!'

His grey eyes gleamed with amusement. 'I enjoyed myself—I had no ties and life was for living,' he admitted, then paused for a second before saying lightly,

'So…I suppose you're married and have kids now. Most of the people I've met back here are in that situation.'

Iona's throat constricted, and she put the mug back very carefully on the table. 'No,' she said shortly. 'Nothing like that.'

Matt gave her a perceptive glance, as if he was aware that he'd touched a nerve. 'So you're fancy-free, then?'

'Oh, yes,' said Iona firmly. 'I'm not tying myself down for a long time.'

'Not met the right one yet?'

'No,' she said lightly. 'Not yet… And you? You've been in Africa, I hear. Your life must have been much more interesting than mine. What were you doing there?'

He smiled at the smooth change of subject. 'I worked for an organisation that assists in child health care in the more remote regions. We used to go out in the field and, besides giving routine health education, we'd see kids who needed acute primary care or referrals—you name it, we did it! It was great, and the children were wonderful!'

His mobile face was alive with enthusiasm, as if by just talking about it he could relive the experience.

'And yet you decided to come home? Was that because you have a family now?' probed Iona, suddenly interested to know why someone who'd loved his job had given it up.

Matt shrugged and finished off his coffee in one gulp. 'No,' he said tersely. 'No wife, no children. Contract was coming to an end and I…well, I thought it was time to come back for, er, family reasons.' He went to the window and looked out at the car park, brightly lit in the dark with security lights, bunching his fists in his pockets.

Iona looked at him sharply. I don't believe him, she thought. Or at least I don't believe that's the main reason he came back to Sellingford. He might seem the most confident guy in the world, but Matt isn't telling the whole truth. She looked at his face. Suddenly it seemed older, sadder, with a rather stricken expression in his eyes. Something had happened to Matt in the three years he'd been away, she was sure of it. Perhaps he was trying to rebuild his life, just as she was.

Iona rose from her chair. 'Back to the grindstone,' she said brightly.

Matt stood back to let her get to the door and as she passed he took her arm gently.

'Iona…I think we ought to celebrate our working together again with more than a cup of freshly brewed coffee. How about a meal some time?' His eyes sparkled down at her humorously. 'Perhaps you'd like to see my etchings—or, rather, my photos from Africa!'

He was still holding Iona's arm very lightly, but she felt his touch acutely, intensely conscious of his nearness to her. If she put his cheek to hers she'd feel his late-night stubble, she thought hazily. Suddenly the crazy idea came into her head that if he didn't move soon she'd end up doing something ridiculous, like pressing her lips to his. In her imagination she could almost feel the electricity that would flicker between them when she felt his mouth touching hers. Matt's face swam into view through her reverie and she realised he was still looking at her, waiting for an answer, one eyebrow raised.

She gave an embarrassed laugh, and said rather

breathlessly, 'Sure, a meal some time…that would be good.'

Immediately she felt annoyed with herself. She shouldn't have been so eager in her response—but anything to get him out of the way, and back to the reality of A and E!

'That's great. I'll organise it. And now there's something I've got to do, been longing to do all evening…'

She looked at him apprehensively. 'What have you got to do?'

He grinned at her, his eyes dancing. 'This!'

He put up his hand and pulled off her hospital cap, which kept her hair out of the way, and smiled as her long thick hair tumbled about her shoulders, a russet silken mane shot with golden highlights.

He let out a long exhalation of breath. 'Ah, that's more like it, Dr Bellamy! I was terrified you might have cut it off,' he declared. 'Now you look as I re-member you—a Renaissance angel!'

He bent his head to hers and brushed her forehead with his lips. 'Here's to some more good times together!'

He turned and marched off down the corridor, and Iona was left staring after him in half angry, half amused astonishment, the feel of his lips imprinted on her skin like a firebrand, her heart fluttering wildly against her ribs.

Sister Bet Lucas, large and imposing, bore down on Iona, who was still trying to pin up her hair under her cap. Sister Lucas had a slightly intimidating air which didn't go amiss in a department like this, and did not believe in what she called disparagingly 'the modern casual way' of addressing staff by their first names. To her, discipline was helped by addressing everyone by their formal titles. She looked curiously at Iona for a second.

'Ah, Dr Bellamy, you all right? You look a little flustered.'

Iona's cheeks coloured slightly. 'No…no, just tidying myself up a little.'

'Good, good—must keep standards up. Now…' Sister Lucas's voice was brisk. 'There's a little girl in cubicle three. Could you look at her, please? Query broken arm.' She dropped her voice slightly. 'I'm afraid the mother's being a little difficult—not improving the situation. Student nurse Brogan's with them now.'

Lucy Brogan's anxious young face was peering round the cubicle curtain as Iona walked up.

'I'm glad you've come,' she whispered. 'Mrs Burford seems very angry. I don't know what to say to her…'

Iona opened the curtains and smiled in amused delight at the little girl sitting up in the bed before her. Polly was a curly-haired blonde child, wearing a little pink tutu with layers of tulle bunching out from her waist, two stiff little wings over her shoulders and a sparkling crown tipped rather crookedly on her head. Her scared big blue eyes looked mournful, but she attempted a shy little smile when Iona spoke to her.

'So you're Polly, are you? My—you do look lovely! I didn't know I'd be trying to make a little fairy better today!'

'I'm the sugar plum fairy,' she whispered. 'But my arm hurts a lot!'

'Well, I'm Dr Bellamy and we'll get your arm sorted out very soon.'

'About time you did!' said a deep throaty voice from the woman at the side of the bed. Slanting, heavily mascara'd green eyes regarded Iona belligerently. 'We've been waiting here for simply *hours*! I brought Polly in ages ago and, of course, by the time we've finished here, the party will be over!'

Iona raised her eyebrows. 'I'm sorry, Mrs Burford—sorry that your little girl has had to wait. Unfortunately we've had a rather busy night here with some major emergencies coming in—and, of course, life-and-death cases are a priority, as I'm sure you realise!'

She smiled politely at Polly's mother, who grimaced and shook her head irritably. 'Oh, I know you medics all complain you're overworked…but it's the same old story, isn't it? Disorganisation! Surely it shouldn't take all this time to have a child seen to. However, I suppose we must put up with bad service!'

Mrs Burford sighed heavily and leant back in her chair, tapping long red fingernails on the locker at the side of the bed. Iona looked at her silently and decided that the woman had the spoilt air of someone who was used to being pampered. Elegant, with a long black coat trimmed with fake fur, Mrs Burford could have stepped out of the pages of a glossy magazine. As she leant back, Iona could tell she was heavily pregnant.

'In fact, Mrs Burford,' Iona said, looking at Polly's notes, 'I see from the time sheet that Polly was X-rayed almost as soon as she came in, and that you had to go and make a phone call after that, having said that you specifically wanted to see the doctor when Polly was being assessed.'

Mrs Burford shrugged. 'So, she's had an X-ray done—where does that get us?'

Iona hooked up the film in front of the viewing light and looked carefully at the image. 'Polly's got a small crack of her radius. The nurse will put a plaster on it to immobilise the arm and it should be quite better in a few weeks.' She turned kindly to the little girl. 'How did you do it, Polly?'

'On a bouncy castle,' whispered Polly. 'I fell into someone…'

'It was a golden wedding anniversary party,' said Mrs Burford crossly. 'They made the mistake of asking all these children—quite silly. There were masses of them on this bouncy castle thing. I could probably sue them for Polly's injury. We're due to go to the West Indies soon and I don't fancy taking a child with a broken arm!'

Little Polly looked stricken. 'You won't leave me behind, will you, Mummy?' she asked mournfully.

'The staff nurse will be here very soon to plaster that arm of yours,' said Iona comfortingly, wondering if the child's mother had an ounce of maternal warmth in her body. 'It won't hurt at all, and then you can go home.'

Iona stroked the little girl's silken hair gently, and reflected wistfully that Mrs Burford didn't seem to appreciate how lucky she was. When she pictured her future, Iona always hoped that children would feature in her life, but somehow that seemed a long way off now. Someone like Polly made those hidden longings surface for a while.

Mrs Burford got up from her chair and put her hand in the small of her back, grimacing slightly.

'They don't make these places very comfortable,' she remarked. 'I feel quite peculiar.'

She opened a beautiful black suede handbag and took out a cigarette, putting it between carmine red lips and snapping a lighter into life in one smooth, practised action.

Iona shook her head. 'I'm sorry, Mrs Burford, this hospital is a non-smoking zone. If you want a cigarette you'll have to go outside.'

The woman stared at her. 'For heaven's sake, we're being completely regimented here!' She sighed heavily. 'Well, I suppose if you insist, I'll have to go out, then. I've got to have something to relax me— these rules and regulations are quite iniquitous. You'll be alright, won't you, Poll? Back soon...'

She began to push her way out of the cubicle, flinging the curtains back in an annoyed manner. Then suddenly she stopped, clutching the curtain with one hand, and gave a small shriek. She turned to Iona, her eyes wide with distress, hugging her enlarged stomach.

'I don't believe it— Oh, no! This can't be happening!'

Iona looked at her in puzzlement. 'Something wrong, Mrs Burford?'

'Only my waters have broken, that's what! I'm about to have my baby!'

If we weren't so busy and short-staffed this might almost be funny, reflected Iona, briskly stepping forward to take the woman's arm and noting with relief that the next cubicle was empty.

'You'll be all right, Mrs Burford,' she said in a firm

voice, trying to calm the agitation she knew the frightened woman would be feeling. 'I want you to come and lie down on the trolley in this cubicle next to Polly's. Someone will come and see you immediately.'

Mrs Burford clutched Iona's hand as a contraction hit her. 'So that's the way to get instant attention here—go into labour,' she muttered through clenched teeth.

A surge of laughter threatened to spill out of Iona—she had to admire the woman for her caustic comment even in the state she was in! As they went out, Iona turned to Polly, who was looking with frightened eyes at her disappearing mother and the sudden confusion that seemed to have arisen around her.

'I'll be back in a minute, sweetheart,' promised Iona reassuringly. 'Your mummy's a bit tired—she's just going to lie down in the cubicle next to yours.'

No one could say A and E was boring, she thought wryly as she helped Mrs Burford onto the bed, but it wasn't often that someone came in with a patient and ended up being a patient themselves! To Iona's relief Matt was walking down the corridor, talking to Bet Lucas. She went up to them rather breathlessly.

'Sister Lucas, Matt—we have a small problem here. My patient's mother has gone into labour very suddenly and the contractions seem rather fierce— every five minutes, I think. Could you just look at her while I see to her little girl and find someone to plaster her arm? We'd better ring Maternity and tell them they've got a referral!'

Matt's eyebrows shot up his forehead. 'Never a dull moment, eh, Sister? If we're not quick we might have an extra small patient we didn't bargain for! Shall I take this one?'

Bet smiled thinly, then pursed her lips. 'If we get a major RTA on top of this I'll have to get some nurses from Medical—there's just not enough of us to go round!'

A loud moan came from the behind the curtains and Matt went into the cubicle. Iona heard his soothing, calm voice. 'A bit of a shock for you, Mrs Burford—but, don't worry, you're literally three minutes away from the delivery suite. Even a baby in a hurry couldn't get here that quickly!'

'Don't be so darn sure!' Mrs Burford's voice was high with an edge of panic in it. 'Polly came in the taxi on the way to the hospital. This one's nearly here—I can feel it!'

Iona went into Polly's cubicle, thankful that Jan was with the little girl already, preparing to plaster her arm.

'Jan,' she whispered urgently in the nurse's ear, 'can you shunt Polly to another place at the end of the corridor? I don't want her frightened by what's going on next door...'

Jan nodded, understanding the situation at once. 'You know, sweetheart,' she said to the little girl, who was now looking rather tearful, 'we've got some lovely toys in the children's room—would you like to come and see them and I'll do your arm there?'

She picked up the child and placed her in a wheelchair tucked by the bed, and with a wink at Iona walked out briskly. 'This little fairy and I are going to fly off to see some special things,' she said.

It was all go in Mrs Burford's cubicle—Iona could

see that things were progressing faster than Matt had anticipated.

He looked round as she came in. 'I'm going to take Mrs Burford up now myself,' he said in a low voice. 'There don't seem to be any porters in sight. Don't they have them in this hospital?'

'Bad night for porters,' admitted Iona. 'I'll come up with you. Have you told Maternity?'

'Yup—the delivery suite's ready so let's go. Hang on there, Mrs Burford!'

The prospective mother gritted her teeth and arched her back. 'I want an epidural,' she shouted. 'Where's the anaesthetist?'

'I think, Mrs Burford,' he murmured, 'you're just a little late for that!'

Matt practically ran along the corridor, pushing the trolley in front of him, Iona trotting by the side, holding Mrs Burford's hand.

'Seven pounds three ounces,' announced the midwife, taking the newborn baby off the scales and handing him to his mother. 'A lovely little boy—and one of the quickest births I've ever seen!'

Mrs Burford lay back on the pillows and looked down at her new son. 'Thank heaven it's a boy,' she murmured. 'Now I can call a halt!'

Her hard face softened and she bent down to place a kiss on the child's forehead, then she flicked a glance up at Matt and Iona standing by the side of the bed.

'Thank you for getting me here so quickly,' she said gruffly. 'I didn't want to have him in the hospital corridor!' She looked down at the new arrival again and a tender smile curved her lips. 'He's not bad, is

he? Will someone let my husband know that Percival
Montgomery Burford has arrived?'

Iona stepped forward, a lump in her throat, and
stroked the baby's soft cheek. It had been some time
since she'd assisted at a confinement, but the experience always left her deeply moved and she was relieved to see that even such a tough mother as Mrs
Burford melted when she had her newborn baby in
her arms.

'He's absolutely lovely,' said Iona admiringly.
'And I think he's going to be blonde like Polly. Won't
she be excited?'

'Oh, heavens, poor little Poll! Left alone with a
broken arm.' Mrs Burford looked slightly stricken.
'What's happened to her?'

'Don't worry,' soothed Matt. 'She's being looked
after by two nurses who are quite enchanted by her.
When you've been taken to the ward, I dare say she'll
be allowed to come and see you both for a few
minutes.' He looked down at the baby with a soft
expression on his face. 'What a beautiful child—
you've done brilliantly! Came in with one child, go
out with two!'

He looked at Iona. 'I think we've done our bit
here—time to make a quick exit!'

They walked back to Casualty together, a sudden
overwhelming tiredness seizing Iona as it often did at
this hour in the early morning. She hardly bothered
to disguise the huge yawn that overtook her. Matt
glanced at her sympathetically.

'Been a hard night, hasn't it? Another coffee?'

She shook her head. 'After I've had a breath of
fresh air outside, perhaps. Bringing babies into the

world is darn tiring—and I don't just mean for the mother!'

He opened the side door into the car park. 'Here we are, then—breathe in some oxygen!'

The fresh air hit her like a douche of water, shocking her senses alive again. Matt smiled down at her.

'That better?' He looked up at the dark, clear sky, alive with stars, and the sweet scent of a balmy summer's night mixed with new-mown grass filled the air. 'There's nowhere like an English summer night,' he murmured, 'even if we are in a hospital car park. It's nice to be back!'

Iona looked up at him. 'Is it? You don't miss the African smells, the beauty there?'

'Some things perhaps, but it's good to be home—for all sorts of reasons!' He laughed suddenly, and put his hand under her chin, lifting her face to his. 'Who would have thought we'd have ended up at Sellingford General together? I never dreamed we'd bump into each other again...'

Iona shifted uneasily from his gaze, aware of her pulse bounding into overdrive at his nearness, alone in the night together. She, too, had never dreamed that Matt Carter would come back into her life. She'd long ago tried to dismiss him from her mind, and now—just when she was trying to get her life into some sort of order—he'd appeared again! And the awful thing was, she heard a little voice whisper in her head, she felt every bit as attracted to him as she had three years ago!

She closed her eyes briefly. If only she could ignore those clear grey eyes, that lopsided, heart-stopping grin and try to forget what it had felt like, having his hard muscular body pressed to hers when they'd danced, try not to imagine what it would be like to feel it against her again! What are you like, Iona? she whispered to herself, shocked by her own thoughts. Men were off limits, weren't they? Especially men like Matt!

'I must get back to the unit,' she said abruptly. 'They're probably stretched to the limit.'

Something seemed to have happened to her in the last few hours, Iona thought rather hysterically as they walked back in silence together. The evening had started off like most evenings in Casualty, with plenty of incident, but nothing unusual—then suddenly Matt Carter had turned up again and all at once her life was a kaleidoscope of emotions, and it bewildered her.

One thing I do know, she told herself sternly, I am never never going out with that man again—he's been the cause of too much turmoil in my life already. Forget about the looks, she thought savagely, forget about the charm. Matt Carter is only a colleague who likes to flirt—nothing more!

'I'm just going to see what the list is like,' she murmured, and strode briskly away from him to Reception.

Matt watched Iona's slender figure disappear through the swing doors. She was just as beautiful as he remembered. Her hair was still that vibrant titian auburn that went with a creamy skin and large hazel eyes—no wonder he hadn't been able to take his eyes off her when they'd worked together. He smiled drily to himself. She'd been a very hard nut to crack when it had come to getting a date three years ago—he'd begun to think she'd never go out with him, and had been amazed when eventually she'd agreed.

He gazed unseeingly at the floor for a second, re-membering that crazy, marvellous evening, the feel of her soft cheek against his when they'd danced, and later on their feverish kisses. After that night he hadn't been able to get her out of his head, even though he'd not been one to commit himself to a re-lationship—he'd been enjoying life too much! Per-haps that had been why, even after she'd completely bowled him over that evening, he'd been almost re-lieved that he'd arranged to go abroad a few days later on an open-ended contract. Iona Bellamy had been a little different to most of the girls he'd taken out—rather special, and possibly in the danger zone when it had come to something more permanent than a ca-sual affair!

No one had known he was going. He'd needed to get away for a while, away from the powerful father whom he loved but who liked to dominate every as-pect of his life. It had taken a while, but eventually he'd managed to put Iona safely out of his mind.

It was a funny old world, thought Matt, a smile lifting his lips. He'd not really been looking forward to coming back to Sellingford, and what had hap-pened in Africa had been tragic and had left him with a raw feeling of guilt—but in one evening the picture had changed, and all at once the future looked much more interesting again!

CHAPTER THREE

TODAY, thought Iona virtuously, flinging open her wardrobe, I am going to throw out half my clothes and sort them into summer and winter. Then I'll tidy out my desk and vacuum round everywhere. She looked at her watch. She hoped she'd have time to do everything before her brother and his boisterous family came for lunch. It was a bank holiday, and she'd already prepared an enormous dish of pasta which could be heated up and served with some French bread and salad. There were also sausages and hamburgers that the children could do on the barbecue—his family had very large appetites!

Glancing up at the window and looking at the sun streaming through, dust motes dancing in a sunbeam, Iona had a moment's regret that she wasn't going for a walk on such a lovely early summer's day like this, her first free day for ages. Then she turned resolutely away—she couldn't put off the grand clear-out any more! She picked out the first item of clothing, a rather shapeless dress in a pretty material, and looked at it doubtfully. Worth hanging onto or binning? Firmly she pushed it into a large plastic bag. No good keeping things just because they might come back into fashion—they never did!

Delving deeper into the wardrobe and dragging out four old evening dresses, Iona caught her breath as she saw one in pale green silk. She picked it up and held it against her, looking at herself in the mirror. It still suited her, the long fitted basque to the waist spilling out in a full skirt, emphasising her small waist and flattering her bust, the soft colour contrasting with her auburn hair. The last time she'd worn this had been three years ago, she mused, at the dance with Matt! She closed her eyes for a second, going back in time, remembering the expression on his face when he'd come to pick her up that evening at her old flat.

'Wow!' he'd said softly, sweeping his eyes over her, 'You look fantastic. That dress is a knockout!'

She'd smiled provocatively at him, confident she'd looked good, and twirled round like a dancer before him. With a broad smile, he'd stepped forward and put his arm round her waist, pulling her closely to him as they'd spun round and round together, so that the dress had swirled out in a green wave round their legs. Iona could still remember the electrifying excitement at the start of that evening and how she'd known it would be a memorable one…

She sighed and dropped the dress on the floor, looking unseeingly out of the window. Just why had Matt got under her skin so much since his arrival back in Sellingford? After all, she'd only been out with him that once a long time ago! Nevertheless he dominated her thoughts, and when they were together her whole being prickled with awareness of him. It was as if, after the unhappiness of the last few months, she'd suddenly remembered just what it was to be really attracted to a man. Matt had awoken feelings she'd tried to bury—and it was getting harder and harder to ignore him.

Iona folded up some jumpers and put them back on a shelf. She was right to keep her distance from Matt, she thought with resolution: treat him as a professional colleague. It was because of him that she'd got entangled with Kevin, and she could never forgive herself for what she'd done to that poor man.

As she flung some old shoes into a box, she reflected pensively that only a few days into the new job Matt hadn't lost his touch, working his magic on all the females. He made things seem fun and light-hearted around him, so that even Bet Lucas, usually so impervious to charm, had melted somewhat in his charismatic presence, going so far as to have coffee with him in her snatched moments of leisure, instead of gulping it down between treating patients. It had to be admitted that it was much more fun going to work than it used to be!

The front doorbell rang stridently in the hall.

Iona looked up impatiently. 'Damn, trust Pete to be early with his crew—I haven't nearly finished yet.'

She glanced at herself in the mirror and shrugged. Her brother and his family would just have to take her as she was—hair pulled up into a knot on the top of her head and a T-shirt over a pair of rather tight pedal-pushers. Luckily, she reflected, Mary, her sister-in-law, was a very easy, informal person who always seemed to dress casually even on occasions when everyone else was dressed to the nines.

'Coming,' she shouted.

She opened the door. Matt stood there, dressed in faded khaki shorts, a white shirt and a wide grin on his lips.

'Great—you're in!' he said to her astonished face. 'I've got a marvellous plan for this lovely day—why don't we have a pub lunch by the river? Short notice, I know…'

'I'm afraid I can't—' Iona began, but he put a hand up in the air as if to stop what she was going to say.

'You know we agreed that one quick coffee in A and E didn't give us enough time to fill in the gaps of our lives since we last worked together, and you said you were on for a meal!'

Iona's eyes widened, a mixture of indignation and excitement making her heart beat a rapid tattoo against her ribs. She'd only just been thinking of the man, and he'd materialised!

'I beg your pardon? I don't remember agreeing to anything, or saying I was free today!'

She tried to sound severe, but a nervous giggle threatened to surface as she marvelled at the man's cheek and his ability to make her heartbeat bound into overdrive. Matt stood in a relaxed way against the doorjamb, dancing grey eyes scrutinising her neat fig-ure and the precarious topknot of her hair—almost enjoying her discomfiture, she thought crossly.

'Oh, yes, you promised all right,' he assured her. 'I would have checked with you earlier about when it would suit you, but you seem to have been very elusive this week.' His voice was smooth. 'I thought I'd just come round on the off-chance. After all, we've both got a day off—pity to spend it inside!'

Iona pulled herself together and said brusquely, 'Could I ask just how your got my address? I thought these things were a private matter!'

'Oh, it wasn't hard,' he said easily. 'The girl in Human Resources is a friend, and when I explained that you and I were old colleagues, she was very co-operative!'

I bet she was, thought Iona. He could wangle in-formation out of anyone!

'I must have a word with her,' she said briskly.

'No harm done,' he said casually, and looked up at the house. 'When did you move here? It's really nice—is it Victorian?'

'I moved about two years ago—and, yes, it's a Victorian terrace house as you can see. Look, I'm sorry,' she said hurriedly, 'but I'm expecting my brother and his family, so...'

There was a sudden kerfuffle behind Matt as a car drew up, sounding its horn. Matt and Iona watched as three boisterous boys spilled out onto the pavement, and a large dog skidded between their legs and bounded up to Iona with yaps of delight.

'Hi, Iona!' Three faces with startling blue eyes and mops of red hair looked up at her and then at Matt.

'Are you coming to lunch, too?' asked the youngest, baldly.

'Hush, boys,' said Mary Bellamy, following her children. 'Stop making such a row.' She smiled in a friendly way at Matt. 'Sorry—a bit of an invasion, I'm afraid.'

There was nothing for it but to introduce Matt to her sister-in-law and then to Pete, although it soon became apparent that they knew each other. Pete was a GP in a small practice out of town and at some stage in his career had evidently met Matt—but, then, Iona thought drily, most people seemed to know him!

They all trooped into the house, Matt going with the flow of people then hanging back in the hall behind everyone for a minute.

'Look, I don't want to intrude. This is a family occasion—I'll come another time.'

Pete put a hand on his arm. 'Hey, none of that. You must stay and help us eat all this food my sister's got for us.' Iona flicked a look of irritation at her brother. He was a kindly man but not overburdened with tact. He continued heedlessly, 'I heard you were back from Africa, and I believe that the charity you worked with is doing sterling stuff out there—I read that vaccinations are up eighty-five per cent in some remote areas. I'd love to hear about it.'

'Can we let Rufus out?' shouted one of the boys.

The adults scattered as the scruffy dog pounded enthusiastically towards the French windows that led out of the hall and bounded into Iona's little walled garden.

'Is he a new acquisition?' Matt grinned.

Mary sighed. 'Against my better judgement. I love dogs, but three naughty boys are enough to cope with at the moment, without training another youngster. He seems to need more exercise than I can give him!'

Iona appeared with a tray of beer, iced lemonade and a bottle of wine.

'Help yourselves, everyone,' she said. 'And let's go into the garden and drink it while the boys start cooking the barbecue stuff.'

They sat on the little terrace, a small apple tree that grew near the house providing shade, and the three children set about happily lighting the barbecue and bickering in a friendly way over what to cook first. Iona took a long sip of wine and flopped down beside Mary, who started telling her about the holiday they all intended to have in France during the school holidays. Iona listened with half an ear, but all the time she was intensely aware of Matt sitting close beside her, his deep voice mingling with Pete's as they discussed work and Matt's African trip. She looked at him covertly under her lashes. He had the relaxed look of someone who could fit in anywhere, any time—a kind of chameleon who took on the hue of his surroundings.

Suddenly Iona realised that the two men were talking about her, and she strained to hear what Pete was saying.

'So you and Iona used to work together three years ago at St Olaf's?' He looked affectionately at his sister. 'Poor old sis! A lot's happened since then, hasn't it, Iona?'

Iona coloured slightly, and Matt looked at her, raising his eyebrows enquiringly. 'Oh? You never told me!'

Mary made a face at her husband, then spoke up quickly. 'Really, Pete! I don't know if Iona wants you talking about her business—after all, that's behind her now.'

'Then she won't mind talking about it,' said Pete comfortably, taking a swig of beer from his can.

Iona filled up Mary's wineglass. 'Nothing to tell really. I was engaged—I'm not now!' Her voice was light but dismissive. 'And now, everyone, I think it's about time we ate. I'll get the salad and pasta—you boys dole out the sausages.'

For the next forty minutes the conversation was general and light, the children making the most noise, the dog leaping around expectantly near the barbecue, waiting for any dropped sausages. Occasionally Matt flicked a glance towards Iona, as if wondering what the full story was behind her bald statement.

The boys began to kick a football against the wall that surrounded the small garden. Mary stood up resolutely.

'Right, boys—enough! It's time for your match

anyway in about half an hour. We'll wend our way to the park.' She smiled rather wearily at Iona and Matt. 'You'll be glad to hear that they belong to a small league in the village and there's a football match this afternoon, which Pete and I are going to help supervise, for our sins. Thank heaven, it's the last match of the season.'

Matt stood up. 'What's going to happen to the dog?' he said.

Mary shrugged her shoulders. 'He'll roar round and round the field, I suppose—can't really keep him in the car all afternoon.'

Matt grinned. 'I'm great with wild animals! Why don't Iona and I take him a walk and get rid of some of his energy—that would be good, wouldn't it?' he said, looking across at Iona.

A walk? Alone with Matt? 'Well,' she said doubtfully, 'I...er...'

'We'd be really grateful, sis!' declared Pete. 'It's bad enough having to keep our eyes on these three at a football match, not to mention dealing with aggressive parents who all think their little darlings should be on the winning side! Looking after Rufus would be one terrific good deed!'

The family gathered themselves together and squeezed into the car.

'Thanks for a lovely lunch,' said Mary, giving Iona a kiss. 'See you later when you bring back the dog to the football match. By the way,' she said, lowering her voice, 'I like your friend. Is he attached?'

'I've no idea,' rejoined Iona crisply, 'He'd only dropped by to, er, tell me something—he wasn't meant to stay for lunch!' Wryly she thought that it hadn't taken Mary long to succumb to Matt's charms!

*   *   *

Down by the river path it was hot and still. Hanging over the water were dragonflies and there was a background murmur of bees as they buzzed busily through the clover and wild roses in the hedge by the path. Iona took in a deep breath and started to relax. It felt good to be out, stretching one's legs and smelling some sweet country air after the aseptic atmosphere of the hospital.

She watched Matt, ahead of her on the path and throwing sticks energetically into the water for Rufus. Matt had a powerful and athletic physique and it seemed no effort to him to throw large pieces of timber miles away. Watching him striding ahead in old khaki shorts and shirt, it was easy to picture him in the wilds of Africa.

Matt turned round and waited for Iona, a slight breeze ruffling his hair. 'This is the hottest day we've had yet,' he remarked. 'I'm absolutely dripping. It's more like Africa than I thought, here! I'll have to take this off—do you mind?'

'Of course not,' murmured Iona, trying to ignore the sight of his muscular tanned chest as he started to pull off his white shirt. She wondered crossly why she was so affected by the sight of his bare chest when it was something she saw every day in Casualty. But, then, most men's torsos didn't look like Matt Carter's, she reflected wryly.

'So,' he said, knotting the shirt round his shoulders and starting to walk beside her, 'tell me about this engagement of yours. Anyone I know—or don't you want to talk about it?' His voice was soft, sympathetic.

'No, you wouldn't know him—and there's nothing

much to tell. After all, people break engagements all the time!'

He nodded. 'That's true. If you're not right for each other, it's pointless going on.' He was silent for a second, then said very firmly, 'No good being tied down for life to someone you don't love—that must be hell. That's why commitment is such a big step. Look before you leap!'

Iona looked at him quizzically. 'So you don't intend to settle down, then, have a family?'

He shook his head and said lightly, 'Not yet awhile. I've got a lot of living to do yet!'

Iona laughed, but she felt a tinge of disappointment because she couldn't help but wonder wistfully if one day Matt would change his ways and need someone permanently! Silly really—she was a fine one to hope for commitment when she'd broken one man's heart and humiliated him. She would never forgive herself for that.

It was as if Matt sensed her underlying sadness as he took her hand and squeezed it. 'It was hard, eh? Still getting over it?'

Iona's hand felt as if she'd suddenly grasped a live electric wire—her hand tingled in his grasp—and yet there was a sort of comforting strength there that she appreciated. She pulled it gently away.

'It…it wasn't a good time for me—but, yes, as my brother said, it's behind me now.'

'That's good.' Matt looked down at her, a rather shadowed expression on his face. 'Sometimes these things work out for the best.'

His mood seemed to have altered somewhat, the usual bright spirit slightly subdued. Matt had a darker side to him, reflected Iona, darting a quick look at his sombre face. She tried a change of subject.

'What made you decide to go to Africa?' she enquired. 'You never mentioned it to any of us when we worked at St Olaf's.'

He shrugged. 'It was rather a quick decision. I needed to get away for certain reasons, and the chance came along to do something exciting and different, away from a hospital for a while.' He gave a short laugh, 'Although in some ways it was very like Casualty. One had to try one's hand at anything that came along, from dysentery to snake bites and lion maulings!'

Iona raised her eyebrows. 'Not many of those round here, but it sounds very exciting. Coming back to Sellingford must be rather dull—did you decide you'd had enough?'

A look of sadness crossed his face, and he stared at the ground. 'Things changed. It wasn't the same and I felt I couldn't stay on.'

He didn't elaborate and, much as she was longing to hear more about his past, Iona felt that she had strayed once more into forbidden territory. She gave an inward shrug. So, he had things in his life he'd rather keep to himself. So did she—there was nothing wrong in that.

His expression changed and he gave one of his devastating grins. 'As for Sellingford being dull, I can assure you that it seems a most interesting place to me at the moment—for all sorts of reasons!'

He gave her a look so intimate and searching that Iona felt her cheeks burning. She didn't know just what he meant by that remark, but she felt slightly flustered, confused by the messages he seemed to be sending out.

'That's good—good that you're enjoying it.' she said lamely.

'You know,' Matt said, stopping on the path and tilting her head up to look at him, 'I've been thinking about that dance we went to before we went away— do you remember it?'

Iona's heart fluttered. 'Sure,' she said lightly. 'It was fun!'

'Perhaps we could do that again. What do you say?'

'Possibly…' Her voice was cautious, remembering her previous resolution not to go out with him. How easy it would be to fall for this man again—and how easy it would be for him to disappear again in his easygoing way without a thought for her feelings.

'You don't seem very sure. I want a more positive answer than that!'

His eyes burned into her, his face so close to hers that she could see the dark flecks in the grey of his eyes, his fringe of black lashes and smell the clean male smell of aftershave. She closed her eyes for a second, trying to push out of her mind the sudden longing to feel his arms pressing her body to his and his lips burning hers—why the hell had she agreed to go for a walk with this darn man?

She shook herself mentally. What had got into her? She'd thought she'd learned her lesson over the past few years. Now suddenly it was as if all restraint had left her, just because Matt Carter, curse him, was standing too close to her, a man who'd just admitted that commitment to any woman was a long way down the line for him.

'You all right, Iona?' he said softly. His hands were on her shoulders and he was looking down at her with concern. 'You've gone a bit pale.'

Her eyes flew open. 'Of…of course. I've never felt better—just a little hot, that's all.'

Their eyes locked for a long second, then he pulled her towards him in a companionable hug.

'You know something, Iona?' he said softly, 'You're a very sweet person. I'm so glad I got the job at Sellingford.'

She shivered with longing. That tantalising caress made her realise just how much she needed to love and be loved, but if she wasn't careful she'd end up with the wrong man again!

A distant sound of barking made them both look at each other in consternation and say in unison, 'Rufus!'

'I'd forgotten about the dog,' said Matt ruefully. 'Other things on my mind, I guess. Where the hell has he gone?'

Iona panted behind him as he ran off down the path, praying that she wouldn't have to go back to her nephews with the news that they'd lost their precious dog! Ahead of her she could hear the sound of splashing and yapping, and as they turned the bend in the river they saw Rufus being borne downstream with a huge stick in his mouth.

'Oh, no. What can we do?' shrieked Iona. 'The silly dog's being pulled along. If he dropped the stick, he might have more chance!'

Matt started galloping along the path until he was well ahead of the dog, then he kicked off his trainers and plunged into the water, grabbing hold of Rufus's collar as the animal swept by him. The current was quite strong and dragging back a big dog against it was going to be hard. Iona also began running until she came to a bend in the river that slowed Matt and the dog down a little. Without giving herself time to ponder the situation, Iona waded into the shallows and caught Matt's hand, holding onto a willow branch as an anchor with her other hand. Gradually Matt made his way back to the river's edge and hauled the dog onto dry land. Iona and he both sprawled on the bank, dripping wet and exhausted.

Matt looked across at her and laughed. His hair was plastered to his head and rivulets of water ran down his face. 'What a couple! I reckon that both of us and the dog have had enough exercise for today—perhaps we'd better return Rufus to the football match before we lose him again!'

'I'm with you there,' said Iona, getting slowly up and looking down in dismay at her dripping pedal-pushers and T-shirt, now clinging very tightly over her breasts. I look like I've been in a wet T-shirt competition, she thought wryly.

'I'll have to go back and change,' she said. 'What about you, Matt?'

He shook his head. 'I'm OK. It's hot, and I'm used to plunging in and out of rivers—not, I have to say, in England!' He flicked a cheeky look over her body and grinned. 'Don't change on my account—from where I'm standing, you look very attractive!'

She made a face at him and, grabbing the dog by the collar, started walking back towards her house.

Matt stopped for a minute, watching her petite figure as she disappeared round the corner, and shook his head almost in bewilderment. He felt as if he'd been hit in the solar plexus. Iona Bellamy was a knockout, and he hadn't expected to feel this way about anyone so quickly after returning home. He knew the danger of falling for her was very real, and he would have to be very careful. Iona had been hurt once, and what right had he to form a permanent relationship after what had happened?

He gazed sadly at the river tumbling past him and, as so often happened, a terrible picture of a car slewed across a road, with the body of a young girl lying beside it, came vividly into his mind. The image was graphic, distinct in every detail—even the silence after the noise of the crash added to the horror. He hadn't been the driver, he hadn't even been near, but he felt as responsible for her death as if he had been at the wheel. Surely it would be wrong for him to take up with someone again when he'd had such a disaster before?

He started to walk slowly towards Iona's house. Perhaps he was a fool to think that he could ever commit himself, and yet he couldn't get Iona out of his head. He sighed. He didn't deserve someone like her, and in any case she'd made it very clear that she wasn't for settling down!

CHAPTER FOUR

'WE'LL give Barry some lignocaine, then I'll start repairing this wound.' Matt's eyes crinkled at Iona
above his mask. 'Glad you could join us, Dr
Bellamy—I thought I was going to have to soldier on
by myself. A bit chaotic out there, is it?'

'You could say that,' said Iona ruefully, trying to
ignore the effect his dancing grey eyes had on her
concentration. 'Jan Fielding and another staff nurse
have gone to help with a multiple RTA on the motorway—bit of a staff shortage at the moment!'

She couldn't help flicking a glance at Matt as he
bent over to inspect the injury of the patient on the
bed before them. If anyone had been looking for a
man to play the part of a surgeon in a hospital drama,
Dr Carter would surely fit the bill! The green tunic
he wore seemed to emphasise his broad frame, the
open ties at the top revealing a cluster of dark hairs
at the base of his neck. No wonder her heart clattered
uncomfortably against her ribs when he was so close
to her, and her thoughts seemed to stray alarmingly
from the matter in hand. In the last few days, the
surge of happiness she often felt rushing through her,
had to be because of her increasing regard for Matt
and the fact they were working together!

Guiltily she forced herself to concentrate and filled
the syringe with lignocaine, a strong local anaesthetic,
before injecting it with a fine-bore needle into the
margins of the wound on the young man's forehead.

It had been a pretty tense morning in A and E, with too few staff, a dearth of porters and nurses and an influx of patients. This patient had been brought in with a nasty dog bite on his cheek and other lacerations, and Iona had been the only one free to assist Matt. The wounds had to be attended to quickly and the plastic surgeon who would normally have looked at it was involved in a long operation with a burns victim.

'You've got some bad bruising round the area of the bite, and that's made your face swell quite a bit, but it should settle down in a few days,' Iona remarked as she looked at the damage done to the man's face. 'You seem to have some other tears on your forehead as well—they don't look like dog bites.'

'I fell against some barbed wire on the fence as I was trying to separate all these dogs,' explained Barry.

'What happened?' asked Matt, checking the array of scalpels and needles on the tray that he would need to use to close up some of the wounds. 'Did they attack you?'

'My dog wouldn't hurt a fly. I was taking him a walk in the park—he's a Doberman—and two Alsatians came up and picked a fight with him.' Barry tried to grin. 'I got caught in the middle, trying to separate them. Warrior didn't mean to bite me—he was trying to defend himself.'

Matt grimaced. 'Pity you got in the way! We need to close these tears from the wire fairly quickly so the tissue doesn't die on us, and the risk of infection is less. Dog bites aren't very clean things so we're swabbing this to get rid of anything nasty, and we tend to leave them open so we don't seal in any nasty bugs. How do you feel?'

'Not bad. Better than I did.'

Matt nodded. The injection of diazepam Barry had received just before he'd come into the little theatre had probably calmed him. It had also acted as a relaxant on his muscles so that it would be easier to work on his face.

'Can you just shine a torch on this torn skin, Dr Bellamy? Let's see how much damage has been done.'

Both doctors looked closely at the wounds. 'One good thing—the periosteum hasn't been pierced,' said Matt.

Iona frowned as she inspected the torn flesh to see if the membrane that covered and nourished the bone beneath had been damaged.

'Yes, you're right—it looks intact to me.'

'Lucky for you, Barry,' observed Matt, and added comfortingly, 'This shouldn't take too long. Keep as still as possible, mate, and I might even get rid of some of your frown lines!'

Matt started to close up the frontalis muscle with the tiny instruments he had to use, cutting away dead skin, using filament gut to stitch the healthy skin. It was a delicate task and any puckering could cause facial distortion. Iona watched in admiration as he completed the suturing.

'All done!' he said at length. 'That was relatively straightforward!' He straightened up and rubbed the small of his back cautiously, getting rid of the stiffness. 'We'll put you into a cubicle for a while to recover, Barry, and send you home later.'

Iona smiled to herself. Matt had made light of the

procedure, but she knew that repairing a wound like that wasn't easy—a lot of skill went into aligning the broken flesh without leaving unsightly scars.

'You should have done plastic surgery,' she remarked.

'Too fiddly for me,' said Matt ruefully. 'Thanks for your help there—we make a good team, don't we?'

He smiled at her as he pulled off his mask and latex gloves, throwing them into the bin. 'By the way, I enjoyed the barbecue last week—it was great, meeting your family.' He paused for a second, his eyes dancing at her. 'I especially enjoyed the walk, even the swim! Perhaps another time we can leave the dog behind. However, we still haven't had that meal together—and you did promise!'

'We had lunch together,' she protested.

'Very nice, but not the same. Too many people around—I want you to myself. How about tonight?'

Iona bit her lip, feeling a mixture of excitement and alarm. She was getting onto dangerous ground again and yet since the barbecue she was beginning to feel more at ease with Matt—which didn't mean that she was any less attracted to him! They'd had some laughs together and there was nothing like a shared sense of humour to relax the atmosphere.

He was watching her intently. 'Go on,' he urged. 'We've got a long day ahead of us—nice to think of something good at the end of it.'

'Just a quick meal, then,' she agreed cautiously.

His mouth twitched. 'We won't stay out all night,' he promised, then added wickedly, 'Unless you want to!'

Iona felt herself turn crimson—the cold truth was that, of course, she wanted to stay out all night with

Matt Carter! She hoped he couldn't read her mind, but ever since that walk, when they'd had to rescue the dog, she'd done too much dreaming about being alone with him, imagining his arms entwined about her, holding her body close to his! She flipped a stray lock back from her forehead, cross with herself for behaving like a schoolgirl besotted by a film star. Then she gave an inward chuckle because wasn't that what Matt looked like—a doctor out of some impossibly romantic film with his open face, firm lips and hard lean body?

He was smiling at her. 'I'll pick you up at your house, then,' he said as they walked from the small theatre towards the main area near the ambulance bay doors.

There was a bustle of controlled chaos at the end of the corridor near the large emergency room where twelve beds were kept in readiness for a major incident. Trolleys, equipment and medical staff were moving in and out of the emergency room with a purposeful air, and Piers Conlan could be seen on the phone, probably warning the orthopaedics department that there could be some patients for surgery later. Both doctors slowed to a halt and Matt gave a low whistle.

'In the meantime, it's obviously back to business,' he commented drily.

'And just when I thought I could grab some of your delicious coffee!' murmured Iona.

Bet Lucas marched towards them, looking grim. 'You've finished dealing with your last patient then? The RTA patients from the crash on the motorway are on their way—three badly injured with suspected compound fractures and back injuries, four with minors. Their ETA is three minutes and the emergency room has been set up.'

Almost as she spoke the sound of an ambulance siren on the drive whined down to silence. The automatic doors swished open a few seconds later and two paramedics came in at a trot with a patient on a trolley, one of them holding up a drip as he ran alongside.

Piers strode beside them, taking details of the patient's state as they panted towards the emergency room. He looked up at Iona.

'You take this one,' he said briskly. 'Matt and I will deal with the others. This is Kevin MacArthur, aged 35, BP 85 over 40 and dropping, pulse 125. Suspected back and neck injury, lacerations to his face.'

Iona stared at Piers incredulously for a moment, hardly hearing the last bit of information.

'What...what did you say the name was?' she said in a cracked, faint voice.

Piers looked at her sharply. 'Kevin MacArthur—do you know him?'

'Yes—yes, I know him.'

'Not a problem, is it? Difficult to switch people around just now...' There was a hint of impatience in his voice—he had a lot of organising to do.

'No...not really. It's just—'

'Then you can put him at his ease!' said Piers genially, as he disappeared to meet the next casualty.

Iona bit her lip. Surely people would understand if she said she didn't want to treat this particular patient? Then she looked back at the entrance and the mass of patients, staff and equipment being marshalled to different places and knew it would be too difficult to change things.

From force of habit she followed the trolley like a robot, although her legs suddenly felt as if they were going to buckle, and her head was dizzy with a range of conflicting emotions. That it should be Kevin who had been brought in badly injured was bad enough. The fact that she was going to deal with him compounded the horror—and how would he feel when he saw his ex-fiancée standing over him?

'Right, everyone,' she said hoarsely, going onto autopilot. 'Let's have this man on the bed. Very carefully, now—suspected spinal injury. One, two, three, lift! We need blood for cross-matching and keep that drip going.'

Kevin lay very still, his neck in a collar. His eyes were open, filmed with pain, his face grey.

Iona took a deep breath and leant over him, 'Hi, Kevin,' she said, with just the vaguest of tremors in her voice. 'It's Iona here. Talk about coincidence! I'm probably the last person you thought you'd see…'

His head remained still, his head anchored by a tape and a neck collar, but his eyes moved to focus on her and widened in amazement. 'Iona? You're dealing with me?' A faint smile twisted his lips. 'Fancy meeting you here! A bit different from last time we were together!'

'I'm sorry,' she said softly, touching his cheek. 'So sorry you've had this accident. I would have hoped we'd have met again in happier circumstances. I'm afraid you'll have to put up with me, unless you've any violent objections?'

'I don't suppose I've got a choice, have I?'

'It would be difficult,' she said briskly. 'Now let's get you sorted.'

Iona shone a small torch into his pupils to test his reactions, then took out her stethoscope and listened to his chest. This was not a time to get emotional, she thought grimly. She had to remain objective, and just get on with the task in hand.

'We're going to make you more comfortable, take some X-rays and give you some painkillers.' She looked up at Jan and a nervous-looking Lucy. 'We need venous access for analgesia, detailed trauma X-rays for spine and neck, legs and feet. Someone get the portable X-ray machine—we don't want to risk moving Kevin.'

She was back in control again, able to think exactly what needed doing. She ran her finger down the arch of his foot. 'Can you feel that, Kevin—and that?'

'I think so,' he muttered. 'My back's damn painful, though.'

'We'll give him five milligrams of diamorphine—that should help.' She added in a low voice to Jan, 'I've got reduced reaction here—could be some neurological damage.'

She bent down to look at the abrasions just under his eye. 'What happened, Kevin—were you driving?'

'No, we were going to a meeting in Liverpool. I remember a lorry coming towards us over the intersection, but not much else.' He couldn't turn his head to look at her, but stared straight up at the ceiling. His voice dropped and he whispered, 'I've missed you so much, Iona, you know. Despite everything, do you think you could ever come back?'

Iona shook her head firmly, but her voice was gentle. 'I'm sorry, Kevin—there's no going back. It wouldn't work, you know.'

Kevin sighed, a tinge of bitterness in his tone. 'You didn't give us a chance, did you? Just walked away. Sometimes I wish I'd never met you. Have you any idea how much you hurt me?' His voice died away.

'I know I did—I went about it the wrong way,' Iona said in a low voice. 'But I did it for the best, Kevin—you'll thank me eventually.'

She felt stricken with remorse and embarrassment, and looked up in relief as Lucy steered in the X-ray equipment, helped by the radiographer.

'We'll get a better picture of your injuries now, Kevin, and see just what treatment you'll need. What are his obs like now, Staff?'

Jan flicked a look up at the oximeter. 'Getting better—pulse 118, BP 85 over 50, sats 95.'

'Right. I'll have a look at those X-rays in a minute.'

She walked out into the corridor and leaned against the wall, her eyes closed, emotionally shattered. This had to be one of the more difficult moments she'd had in Casualty she reflected gloomily.

'Anything the matter?' Matt's deep voice cut into her confused thoughts, and she opened her eyes as he strode past her with a sheaf of X-rays in his hand. He came to a halt and looked at her in concern. 'You look as if you're in shock yourself, never mind the patients! Do you need anything?'

'I'm OK. Something totally unexpected happened and I wasn't prepared.' Iona gave a watery smile. 'I've been caught off balance, I suppose—and I've just handled something rather badly!'

Matt raised one eyebrow questioningly. 'Sounds intriguing. Perhaps you'll tell me about it later.'

'Perhaps…' She sighed and stood up straighter. 'Must get back, see what my patient's X-rays reveal about his spine.'

The radiologist had hooked up Kevin's X-ray in front of the viewing screen and turned to Iona as she came into the room.

'Kevin's fractured a bone in his lumbar spine—L2,' she said, pointing to the afflicted area on the picture.

Iona grimaced. 'I'll get Mr Donaldson, the neurosurgeon, to have a look at him—he may need an operation. Anything else there?'

'I can't see anything untoward in the upper spine or neck. I reckon he's had a lucky escape.'

'His BP's settling down, so hopefully there's no internal bleeding. I'll go and see what the bed situation's like.'

As she passed by the bed, Kevin put out a hand and touched her. 'How bad is it?' he whispered.

'The good news is you'll heal eventually, but it will take a few weeks. You've fractured a bone in the lower part of your spine and that could mean an operation, I'm afraid.'

'A pity you can't heal broken hearts here,' Kevin said sadly, and Iona bit her lip. What she'd done had been for the best—for both of them.

Somehow a cloud fell over the rest of the day. Seeing Kevin again had unsettled Iona, bringing back feelings of pity for the man, mixed with relief that she'd had the courage to break off their engagement. He was a nice man—but he wasn't for her. She'd only to contrast what she felt for Matt after a few weeks to realise that sparks had never crackled between

Kevin and herself. When Matt was near it was as if a small thunderbolt had exploded inside her—every single nerve seemed to tingle and all she could think were quite unsuitable thoughts about what she'd love him to do to her, and her to him!

And yet, she'd reflected sombrely, hadn't she once thought she was in love with Kevin? It had been a pale sort of love compared to her feelings for Matt, but nevertheless it had seemed genuine at the time.

Fortunately they were too busy for her to dwell at length on her guilt about Kevin—it just hovered like a little sad mist at the back of her mind. She almost welcomed the distraction of work. 'Iona! Can you come here quickly? There's a bit of a drama in Reception. A lady's been brought in and she's bleeding badly…'

Connie, the receptionist, peered with frightened eyes round the door of the office where Iona was updating patient information on the computer. 'There's an awful lot of blood. It's…it's pouring all over the floor,' she said dramatically, an edge of panic in her voice.

'OK—I'm with you.' Iona sprang to her feet. 'Find Colin—he's probably outside, having a smoke. Tell him to bring a trolley to the front quickly.'

Connie dashed off looking uncharacteristically scared, and Iona made her way to Reception. Lucy was trying to help a middle-aged woman to a chair, whilst the few people waiting watched in horrified fascination. The patient was white-faced, and blood seemed to be gushing from her leg, forming a pool on the floor. A small man stood helplessly at her side, twisting a cap in his hands.

'You'll be all right, Doris,' he said in a nervous, squeaky voice. 'They'll know what to do here!'

'What's happened?' asked Iona, bending down to look at the woman's leg.

'This is Doris Ecclestone,' said Lucy in a rather shaky voice. 'She fell over a coffee-table and cut her leg on the corner...'

'Right—where's that trolley? We need to elevate this leg and apply pressure to the wound. I think Mrs Ecclestone's cut a varicose vein—that's why it's bleeding so profusely,' said Iona briskly. She smiled reassuringly at the woman who lay back in the chair with half-closed eyes. 'Don't worry, Mrs Ecclestone—we'll sort it out for you.'

Lucy's face had gone almost as parchment white as the patient's. She had only started her course a few weeks before and seemed very nervous and unsure of herself.

Iona flicked a look of concern at her. 'Lucy, are you OK?' Lucy nodded speechlessly. 'Then go and hurry Colin up with that trolley now!'

Lucy turned to go, then put her hand up to her forehead and very slowly sank to the ground in a dead faint. This, thought Iona grimly, is all I need! She stood up and in one smooth movement pushed a chair under Mrs Ecclestone's affected leg, whilst calling in as calm a voice as possible for someone to come and help her—now!

Jan and Colin, the amiable but slow porter, both appeared at once, closely followed by Matt. Together the three of them managed to transfer the patient to the trolley and she was whisked off to the emergency room. Mr Ecclestone's little figure bobbed behind them, still murmuring, 'You'll be all right, Doris. You're in the hands of experts, don't worry!'

Matt turned to help Lucy, leading her, dazed and embarrassed, to the kitchen. As they walked behind Iona, she could hear his soothing voice comforting the young girl, well aware how distressed she was feeling.

'What you need, Lucy, is a nice hot cup of sweet tea,' he said firmly. 'You'll feel better then.'

'I feel terrible now,' said the young nurse tearfully. 'Fancy letting everybody down—it was the sight of all that blood. Perhaps I'm in the wrong job!'

'Nonsense. Lots of students feel peculiar at first when they see something like that. You're certainly not the first one—in a few months you'll be so used to it you won't turn a hair, I promise you!' He smiled reassuringly at her. 'To be truthful, when I first started I was very wobbly when I saw lots of blood. I'm much better now, unless it's my own! A little tip—if you feel peculiar again, just sit down and lower your head. Works like a charm!'

Iona glanced behind her and saw Lucy give a grateful, tremulous smile at Matt. How tactfully he'd dealt with the student nurse, making her feel she'd done nothing too terrible and giving her the courage not to give up with a few kind words. Brogan would probably always be grateful to Matt.

In the emergency room Iona elevated Mrs Ecclestone's leg, and Jan pressed the wound firmly with a large sterile gauze pad.

'This lady's BP's rather low, 80 over 50, and she's lost quite a lot blood,' murmured Jan.

'We'll cross-match her blood, then get supplies. In

the meantime, we'll give her some haemacel—she needs to make up the fluid she's lost.'

'You can't give her blood!' said a squeaky voice behind them.

Iona and Jan turned to look in surprise at Mr Ecclestone, who was standing in the corner of the room, still twisting his cap.

'We may need to,' said Iona gently to the agitated little man. 'Your wife's in shock and her blood pressure's very low.'

'You still can't give it her,' he said stubbornly. 'She won't have it. She's got very strong views on interfering with nature—we both believe it's wrong to accept someone else's blood.'

'We have to respect her wishes, of course, Mr Ecclestone, but it could have serious repercussions...'

'It doesn't matter,' he insisted. He looked tremblingly at his wife, lying white-faced on the bed, and she nodded back to him. He continued more resolutely. 'It's true, isn't it, Doris? No matter what the consequences, we feel very strongly about it.'

Iona inclined her head. It was just one of the many unforeseen aspects of medicine that were thrown up before the staff every day, and had to be dealt with understandingly.

'I see. Then we'll have to do our best. I take it she'll accept plasma substitute—that is, a man-made substance? She really needs the volume of liquid increased to make up for the loss of blood.'

Mr Ecclestone pursed his lips judiciously. 'Yes, we'd have no objection to that.'

Jan set up the drip pole and Mrs Ecclestone began to receive the haemacel.

'Let's keep our fingers crossed that this does the

trick,' murmured Iona to Jan. She put a weary hand up to her forehead. 'There seem to be too many complicated cases today—I think I'm getting a headache!'

Piers came into the room. He looked tired, but he maintained an air of geniality and calmness, even after a horrendous morning coping with the major traffic incident.

'I'll take over here,' he said. 'You go and snatch a bite to eat. I'm in a meeting this afternoon, so you can get your lunch now. I'll bleep you if you're needed.'

'Thanks Mr Conlan—Staff will fill you in regarding Mrs Ecclestone's case.'

Piers smiled reassuringly at Mrs Ecclestone and her husband and said kindly, 'Let's see how you're progressing, Mrs Ecclestone. You've had a nasty shock, but this does happen from time to time when varicose veins get a bad knock...'

His voice was just as soothing and concerned as it had been from the very first patient that morning. He knew the value of removing apprehension from a patient, and how reassurance was as good as a clinical tool. In that respect, reflected Iona as she walked to the cafeteria, Matt was very like him. Patients co-operated with Matt because they knew he was in control and they felt safe.

Iona looked round the cafeteria—as usual it was heaving with staff and visitors, but at the far end someone was waving to her to join them. She bought a sandwich and coffee, and made her way over, wrinkling her nose at the familiar smell of boiled cabbage mixed with hamburger that seemed to permeate the room.

'Chloe—how lovely to see you!' she said, sinking

gratefully into a chair and stretching out her legs. 'I knew you were around, but I haven't had time to draw breath this morning.' She looked at her friend quizzically. 'I haven't seen you since your date—I'm dying to know how it went.'

Chloe gave an impish smile and put up a triumphant thumb. 'Blissful—he's the business!' she announced. 'I think it was your dress that did it—he was completely smitten! Jeremy could be just the man I'm looking for—plenty of money, moves in all the best circles and he's desperate to settle down!'

Iona laughed. 'You don't mean all that, you wretch!'

Chloe waved a large cheese sandwich in her face. 'Sure I do—and so does every other girl, deep down!' She looked at Iona keenly. 'By the way, I saw the new registrar the other day—talk about dishy! I hadn't realised he was Professor Carter's son. Is he married or anything?'

'No—he's not married or "anything", as far as I know.' Iona tried to keep her voice light, and hoped the usual tell-tale signs of a blush wouldn't materialise!

'Wow—there's eligible for you!' said Chloe. 'You know, he's just the sort of man you need, Iona. He looks as if he's got a sense of humour, and he's drop-dead handsome!'

'I've never really noticed,' lied Iona. 'Anyway, I've told you, I'm not in the market for a relationship right now.'

Chloe shook her head sternly at her friend. 'Iona Bellamy—you've got to stop this nonsense of feeling guilty about Kevin and how you can't choose men—it's ridiculous!'

Iona shrugged and gloomily took a sip of coffee. 'You'll never guess what happened this morning,' she said. 'I had Kevin MacCarthur in as an RTA patient!'

Chloe's eyes widened. 'You're joking! That must have been a shock—how did you manage?'

'Not very well—it brought it all back to me. I don't think it did his blood pressure any good having me treat him either! One good thing though, it made me even more certain I'd done the right thing, if not in the right manner—although it shows that my judgement over men isn't all that good.'

'There you are, then!' said Chloe triumphantly. 'Now is the time to move on!' She looked up as someone approached their table. 'Oho!' she muttered in an undertone. 'Talk of the devil!'

Iona felt the hairs on the back of her neck prickle— she knew at once who was standing beside them without having to look up!

'Sorry to interrupt,' said Matt's deep voice. 'Just a quick word with you Iona about tonight. I forgot to say the time I'd pick you up. Is seven-thirty OK?'

He smiled down at her, and Chloe's fascinated curiosity seemed almost tangible. Iona could sense her friend's eyes darting from her to Matt with the deepest interest!

'Yes, sure, I'll be ready,' Iona said lightly.

'I'll look forward to that, then—although it probably won't have the excitement of the other afternoon!'

He raised a hand in farewell and strode off, the eyes of nearly every female in the room following his tall figure with appreciative eyes.

Chloe looked furiously across at Iona. 'How *dare* you, Iona Bellamy? You've been holding out on me,

haven't you? You've known this Dr *Gorgeous* Carter
all along—and, what's more, apparently you've already been out with him!'

'It's not what you think,' protested Iona feebly. 'I
used to know him when I worked at St Olaf's. We're
just mates and we're catching up on old times—that's
all.'

'Mates, indeed!' scoffed Chloe. 'I saw the way he
looked at you—and it wasn't at all like a mate! He
looked as though he could eat you up! There's more
than a "just good friends" scenario between you
two—I can feel it in my bones. I've got extra-sensory
perception!'

Iona giggled. 'He's only a colleague…'

A snort of derisory laughter was the answer and
Chloe stood up, wagging her finger at Iona. 'If I
didn't have the dubious pleasure of going to the
morgue to see the results of a post-mortem, I'd drag
the whole story out of you, Dr Bellamy. Only a colleague indeed!' She gave a mischievous grin. 'Meanwhile, I've got some good advice for you—play it
cool, babe!'

She marched off and Iona shook her head in
amusement. Chloe had a point, however. If Matt was
at all keen on her, she was going to tread carefully.
OK, he made her feel like a shaken jelly when he was
near. She didn't have to wonder if she was attracted
to him—she darn well *knew*! But as for Matt… Perhaps he was just playing along with her as he'd done
with so many—she didn't want to join the long list
of his exes! Nor, she thought, pensively pleating her
paper napkin, did she want to make another mistake.

CHAPTER FIVE

IT WAS a sultry evening with a touch of thunder in the air. Iona took a deep breath and smelt the peculiar tang of electricity that preceded storms, mingled with the sweet fragrance of new-mown grass from her neighbour's garden. She closed her eyes for a second. How lovely to get the hospital smell and noises out of her system for a while!

The house had felt stuffy, closed in, and the knot of nervous anticipation in her stomach at the thought of her evening with Matt seemed to be getting larger every second. Somehow it was more soothing to wait outside. Perhaps she felt jangled up because she'd met Kevin so unexpectedly that day. It seemed to have triggered renewed feelings of guilt and remorse— made her feel it was somehow wrong to go out and enjoy herself with Matt.

Iona glanced appraisingly at the reflection of her-self in the glass of the front door. Was the black silk top with its thin straps and short skirt too skimpy, and did the hint of cleavage send out the wrong signals? She shrugged, irritated with herself that the thought of going out with Matt should send her into a spin about her outfit. She felt cool and comfortable, and just right for a warm summer's evening—except, she thought wryly, for the family of butterflies that was flying round in her stomach!

When Matt's battered little open-topped car drew

up with a squeal of brakes, the butterflies started to turn somersaults!

He jumped out of the car, looking coolly casual in an open-necked shirt and jeans, and leaned against the bonnet of the car for a second, giving her a heart-stopping smile and allowing his gaze to wander over her rather too intimately. Then he walked up the little path and put his hands on her shoulders, an expression of admiration in his warm grey eyes.

'You don't look as if you've been working flat out all day,' he murmured. 'You look as fresh as a daisy.'

Iona laughed. 'My feet know I've been working! It's too hot to wear anything very dressy, so I hope we're not going anywhere formal?'

'Hardly—there's a pub further down the river and they've got tables outside. After the day we've had, it'll be nice to relax.'

He slung an arm casually round her bare shoulder as they walked to the car. She tried to ignore the fact that she could almost feel his bare flesh on hers through his thin shirtsleeves, and the way it made little darts of excitement thrill through every nerve, sending her heartbeat up several notches. She took a deep breath, determined to ignore the way her treacherous body reacted when she was near Matt, and as soon as possible she slipped out of his grasp and ran round to the passenger side of the car.

If he felt slighted, he didn't show it, just followed her briskly and opened the door for her. 'I hope you're hungry,' he said with a grin. 'I don't like girls to pick at their food!'

Iona felt that the last thing her stomach needed was food, but she nodded with false enthusiasm.

'I'll do my best,' she murmured.

*   *   *

The Jolly Miller was crowded with people, but Matt found a table for two tucked away in the corner of the outside terrace, and returned from the bar with a bottle of sparkling white wine.

'I think we deserve this,' he said, pouring them both a large glass each and sitting down opposite her. He held her gaze for a second and raised his glass. 'To our renewed acquaintance, Dr Bellamy,' he murmured. 'May it be long and happy.'

Then he leant back in his chair and looked at her with narrowed eyes. 'And now I want to know more about this morning's mystery, and what happened when you were treating your RTA patient. You seemed a little shocked, to say the least.'

Iona took a refreshing swallow of the wine and felt the bubbles prickle the back of her throat—she could almost feel an instant kick of alcohol on her empty stomach, and it felt good! She smiled ruefully at Matt.

'Too right I had a shock! My patient turned out to be someone I'd parted from in rather difficult circumstances a few months ago. I'd rather not have treated him, but it was too chaotic to get someone to switch patients.'

'So you were very embarrassed?'

'It was awkward,' Iona admitted, and sighed, brushing away a tendril of hair from her eyes. 'You see, Kevin MacArthur is my ex-fiancé—I was hoping I wouldn't bump into him for a long time!'

Matt raised his eyebrows. 'Ah, I see—the man you told me about before? No wonder you had a shock— it must have been an uncomfortable situation.'

Iona looked down at the table, the shadows of her lashes forming arcs on her cheeks. 'I felt terrible,' she said simply. 'You see, I was the one who broke up the relationship. I'd begun to realise early on that he wasn't the one for me. But the way I did it was…cruel, and it was very clear today that he hasn't got over it. He was quite distraught, and it was difficult to know what to say. The poor man had to cope with me—and the fact that he'd fractured a bone in his lumbar spine.'

She gave a shaky laugh, and Matt put his hand across the table, covering her small hand with his. It felt warm and comforting.

'But you did the right thing if you didn't love him. Surely you were being cruel to be kind?' he said.

Iona took another sip of wine and looked across at Matt in a rather stricken way. 'I didn't have to be so cruel—I was cowardly,' she said flatly. 'I left it to the last minute, you see.'

'The last minute?'

She sighed and looked at the reflection of the lights of the pub dancing in the water. 'I mean I literally left poor Kevin standing at the altar,' she said quietly. 'I shouldn't have picked our wedding day to do it.'

There was a short silence between them, and the babble of background noise seemed to grow louder. Matt stared at Iona in astonishment.

'You left it till your *wedding* day to finish it?' he said at last in an incredulous voice.

She nodded miserably. 'Yes… As I said, I was too cowardly to tell him earlier. There never seemed the right opportunity…'

'But the day of the wedding seemed right?' Matt looked at her with disbelief, a cold expression in his eyes. He shook his head. 'I can't believe you could do that to a guy! No wonder the poor man was distraught.'

Iona sensed Matt's disapproval and bit her lip. 'With hindsight, of course, I should never have let it go on so long,' she admitted. 'But every time I thought I'd tell him that we couldn't go on, either he was going for an important interview or he'd had a terrible day...'

'You must have loved him once?'

'I...tried to convince myself I did. I was wrong. One can change, you know. Perhaps I'm just a bad judge of my own emotions. When he started asking me out, it happened at a time when I felt extremely vulnerable.' She looked at Matt rather strangely for a second, then continued, 'Kevin's parents were very good friends of mine, and there was a lot of pressure from both sides to make such a "suitable" match. I think he was unhappy, too. It was a convenient arrangement for us both. We wanted it to work but it just didn't.'

'So you allowed yourself to be swept along by it?'

Iona was suddenly stung by the cold scorn in Matt's grey eyes—eyes that normally held such warmth and laughter in them.

'OK,' she said with revived spirit. 'So I pulled the rug from under him—but better then than after the wedding. And I might add, it took a lot of courage to do it just as I was walking with my father up the aisle! Anyway,' she added, looking at him with a hint of bitterness, 'you don't know the circumstances that made me drift into that situation—you have no right to judge me!'

Matt looked at her flushed cheeks and the tawny eyes sparking across at him. A rueful smile lifted his lips and he shrugged. 'You're absolutely right—I'm the very last one in a position to criticise anyone for making a mess of their love life.' He paused for a second. 'And that's why you said you didn't want to settle down, is it?'

'I don't want to make another mistake like that.'

He nodded. 'I can understand that,' he murmured.

Matt looked at Iona across the table. The dusk was closing in, but a lamp behind her threw a golden glow over her face, emphasising the glorious rich colour of her hair as it spilled over her shoulders. How dark her eyes were, and how creamy soft her complexion! God, but she was beautiful! An intense longing came over him to kiss her full mouth and run his lips down to the tantalising little hollow in her neck, to bury his hands in that thick mane of hair.

The chances of her allowing him to do that were vanishing rapidly, he thought ruefully. How could he have been so pompous as to criticise her for finishing with her fiancé on their wedding day? If his own life was an example, he was a fine one to talk about making mistakes... He twirled his wineglass and watched the bubbles rush to the surface.

'Iona...I'm sorry, I was right out of order there. It's nothing to do with me and, yes, you did a brave thing. It must have been harder to finish things between you at the last moment than it would have been earlier. I'm always opening my big mouth too soon.' He leaned forward and stroked her cheek and looked beseechingly into her eyes. 'Am I forgiven?'

She looked at him stonily for a second, then laughed. He looked so like a little schoolboy, his dark hair sticking up rather spikily round his head, his eyes mournful and pleading.

'I suppose so... And now, are we going to have any of this food you've talked about?'

His eyes danced at her. 'Leave it to me,' he said. 'I'm going to order the lightest, most delicious seafood soufflé you've ever tasted, followed by a mouth-watering raspberry crumble and cream!'

Iona leaned back in her chair. The whirling butterflies in her stomach seemed to have subsided, and suddenly she felt relaxed and realised she was actually enjoying herself with Matt. Perhaps it was the wine, perhaps it was because she'd told him about Kevin—talking about it seemed to have helped put it more into the past. Of course, she reflected wryly, she hadn't told Matt the whole story. There was just one little bit she'd left out—but perhaps she need never reveal that!

The waiter brought them their food, and Iona's appetite returned like magic. She bit appreciatively into the succulent soufflé and it gave a little creamy explosion in her mouth.

'This is lovely—absolutely ambrosial. It's been a long time since lunch!' She looked at Matt rather impishly. 'Now I've given you my life story—it's about time you spilled the beans on yours! Don't tell me there was no one in Africa, because I don't believe you—an eligible bachelor!'

Matt took a long sip of his wine and smiled. 'A penniless doctor is hardly eligible—although I did meet some lovely girls,' he parried lightly, and his eyes twinkled. 'I can honestly say, though, there was no one who could hold a candle to you.'

Iona laughed and said teasingly, 'You've still got all the right lines, haven't you, Matt? You'll get yourself into trouble some day with your honeyed words!'

It was as if she'd switched off a light. Matt's expression changed almost to a look of anguish and his fingers tightened convulsively on the stem of his wineglass. With a sudden crack it broke in half and the wine spilt over the tablecloth. Iona flicked a look of astonishment and concern towards him. Just what had she said to touch a nerve there, to cause such a reaction? Matt had his head down, busying himself patting the patch of wine dry with his napkin, and when he looked up again, his face had regained its composure.

'That was a little careless,' he said, and smiled. 'Now, what about some coffee?'

Iona had opened her mouth to reply when a tremendous roll of thunder and a spatter of sudden rain drowned out her voice completely. In two minutes the spatter had become a cloudburst and the water had burst through the trelliswork above them, soaking them completely. Everyone made a dash for the inside of the pub and soon a steaming crowd of wet people were jostling together in a small space.

'Time to leave, I think,' yelled Matt to her in the noisy atmosphere. 'I'll go and pay now. Why don't you go to the door and wait for me there.'

Iona found herself jammed up against the vast stomach of a man who was so wet he looked as if he'd been swimming. With great difficulty she fought her way round him to the door and peered out into the pouring rain. She could just make out Matt's little car parked down the lane and the fact that the hood hadn't been put up!

Matt's hand took her elbow and he propelled her out of the pub, his face smiling down at her, his teeth gleaming whitely in the dark.

'We'll be all right in the car,' he said brightly. 'I'll put the heater on and we'll soon dry off!'

'You're an optimist,' shouted Iona as they ran down the path. 'We'll be sitting in pools of water!'

Matt stopped suddenly and groaned as he saw the car. 'Oh God, I'd forgotten about the hood! I'll never get it up now—I'm afraid the poor old mechanism doesn't like water. Looks like we'll have rather a wet ride home!' He laughed. 'Who said open-topped cars weren't fun?'

Iona felt that she'd never been wetter—or colder—in her life. The humidity had gone, but the temperature had dropped several degrees and after a five-minute ride in a car open to the elements there wasn't one bit of her that was dry.

Matt looked across at her as they drew up in front of the house, his lips twitching in a smile. 'Never let it be said I don't give a girl a good time,' he murmured. 'I'm really sorry about this…'

She smiled back at him through the teeming rain, looking at his dripping face, his dark hair plastered over his forehead. 'Not your fault,' she said. 'Would…would you like a coffee—or perhaps a whisky?'

'Sure—sounds a great idea.'

Iona suddenly started laughing. 'What on earth do we look like? Absolute drowned rats! We look as if we've been shipwrecked!'

He looked at her silently for a second, then put his hand up and touched her sodden hair, running his finger down her neck to the hollow of her throat. 'You look like a mermaid,' he said huskily. 'A very beautiful mermaid.'

Then he leaned forward, and very deliberately put his hand behind her neck and pulled her face to his. Then his lips came down and brushed hers delicately with the softest of kisses.

It was so totally unexpected that Iona gasped, then the fluttering inside her became a beating pulse and suddenly she couldn't stop herself from twining her arms round his neck and pulling him closer to her, so close she could feel his heart beating against hers. And all the time the rain was lashing down on top of them.

She closed her eyes as his lips fluttered down her neck with butterfly kisses, making every nerve in her body tingle with the excitement of anticipation. His hands caressed her drenched body and she wriggled against him with pleasure. He gave a low laugh.

'I've never had so much fun in the rain before,' he murmured in her ear. Then he leaned back and looked down at her. 'I could do much more justice to our goodnight kiss in a more comfortable place.' He grinned. 'Right now I've got a gearstick pressing into rather a delicate part of my anatomy!'

'Come on, then—let's get dry and warm!'

They scrambled out of the car, the rain stinging their faces and bouncing off the path in little explosions. Iona's hand trembled as she tried to fit the key into the door—and it wasn't just the cold that made her tremble…

Matt switched the hall light on when they came in, and looked down at Iona's shivering form.

'For heaven's sake, go and have a warm shower,' he commanded. 'You'll end up with hypothermia. I'll go and make us some hot coffee and find this whisky of yours!'

'But what about you? You're just as wet as I am.'

'I might just be able to fit into a bathrobe of yours, and I'll put my clothes on a radiator.'

'I can do better than that. Go into the spare room where my brother keeps a change of clothing when he stays here if he has to attend a dinner in town or something.'

Matt nodded. 'Thanks—that sounds more suitable than anything of yours! Now, go on…shoo!'

As Iona stood gratefully under the shower, hot needles of water coaxing her body back to warmth, a mixture of disappointment and relief danced in her mind—disappointment that Matt's kisses had been cut short, and relief that she hadn't had time to let all discretion fly out of the window!

Matt lay back on the sofa with his eyes closed, his long legs splayed in front of him, dressed in Iona's brother's shirt and grey trousers. Was he being a fool to come back for an intimate evening with Iona when every fibre in his body wanted to make love to her, when all he could think of was taking her in his arms and devouring her with kisses? It wasn't just desire he felt for her—he knew that—there was mutual admiration and fun between them also, but when Iona had said, 'You'll get yourself into trouble with your honeyed words,' it had struck a terrible chord. He had to be absolutely sure he wanted commitment—not lead her on—after his last tragic episode.

Iona came in, shutting the door softly behind her, and he opened his eyes, sweeping them over her neat figure, now dressed in a fluffy white bathrobe, her hair spread in damp disarray over her shoulders.

He patted the sofa beside him. 'Come here, Dr

Bellamy, and have some of this wonderful medicine I've just concocted to a secret formula!'

Iona took the glass he offered her and sipped it cautiously. 'Not bad... I can guess at least three ingredients—hot water, whisky and honey. Am I right?'

'Practically.' He grinned. 'I found some blackcurrant juice as well, so I threw some of that in!'

The drink formed a hot path down to her stomach, and Iona began to feel a warm, relaxed glow. She lay back on the sofa and smiled up at Matt, a hint of mischief in her eyes.

'Can you ever put up the hood of your car?' she asked, 'or do you always have to drive with it down, come rain, hail or sleet?'

He laughed ruefully. 'I'm sorry about that. Poor little car, she's not in a good state,' he admitted. 'The trouble is, I can't afford anything else at the moment. I'm buying a cottage just outside Sellingford, and that's rather cleaned me out for the time being. I promise you, I'll have it fixed before I take you out in it again.'

Her eyes danced at him. 'You think I'll risk ruining my clothes and my hair to go in that machine again? I have a feeling whatever you do to that roof it won't be watertight!'

'If we went by taxi, would you risk coming with me to my father's retirement bash? It's being held at my parents' house.' He smiled encouragingly at her. 'Go on—say you will! It would be more fun with you there!'

Prof. Carter, as he was known, was the senior thoracic consultant at the hospital, and all the great and the good would be gathered at such an eminent man's departure.

Iona nodded with enthusiasm. 'I'd enjoy that, Matt. Prof Carter must be delighted you've come back to his hospital—nice for you, too, I guess.'

Matt gave a wry smile. 'I'm very fond of my father, of course, but being so near to him has its disadvantages! He likes to keep an eye on his only son, and he can be rather a bully when he wants his own way—so perhaps I'm relieved he's retiring!' He smiled at her, and an almost resigned expression came in to his eyes, as if he had given in to some inner need. 'Enough about my father!' he said softly.

He turned his body towards her, cupping her face in his hands, and looked at her with such naked longing that her heart began to hammer against her ribs. He was too close, and now that she knew what it felt to be kissed by Matt, she didn't know how she could resist another onslaught. He lifted a lock of her damp hair and put his face down to smell it.

'That smells lovely,' he murmured. He pulled her head back gently and bent his face very close to hers, so that his lips were just a whisper away. 'Now, just where had we got to, before we were so rudely interrupted?' he said huskily.

Then his lips slid down her neck and nuzzled the delicious little hollow in her neck. Iona held her breath, then as he reached the tantalising swell of her breasts beneath the softness of the towelling robe she arched her back against him, revelling in the excitement of his touch. Every erogenous zone in her body tingled as he undid her robe and it fell from her shoulders, leaving her exposed in just her bra and panties.

'You are so beautiful,' he whispered, his eyes devouring the slender curves of her body. 'I didn't plan to kiss you at all—but I can't damn well help myself.'

He trailed his fingers delicately down her stomach, then bent his head to follow that with butterfly kisses until she moaned faintly with longing. Her arms went round his neck and she felt him straddle her body, his powerful frame pressing on hers, his mouth finding hers, teasing it open, exploring its secret places hungrily.

So much for good intentions, thought Iona hazily, as every nerve responded, his expert touch sending delicious little thrills of shock through every limb. Then somewhere an insistent voice in her head began whispering insidiously—was she being a complete idiot all over again, allowing Matt to work his magic on her as he had before? Had she learned nothing from the night she'd gone to the dance with him? Everything seemed to be gathering speed, going far too fast, and she had a feeling that he was just playing the field again!

The sudden ringing of Matt's mobile by the sofa was like a bolt from the blue—and almost a relief. They looked at each other for a second, slightly dazed by being jolted back so quickly from the height of passion into the world of stark reality. Matt groaned and pushed himself from her with a wry grimace, flicking a look at his watch.

'No guesses what this will be at this time of night,' he said tersely. 'Looks like the end of a lovely evening!'

Iona watched his face change expression as he answered the phone. 'Hell,' he said in a low voice. 'Give me ten minutes…and, yes, I'll try and contact her!'

Matt switched off his mobile and turned to her with a resigned look. 'We're both needed,' he said grimly.

'A multiple pile-up involving about fifteen motorcyclists. They want us there to help the paramedics. They're stretched to breaking point dealing with another accident as well—people trapped in a collapsed building at the other side of town. The hospital's on red alert!'

They went straight to the scene in Iona's car as the inside of Matt's was still very wet, although it had stopped raining. Neither of them spoke as they raced there, as if being jolted back to reality had robbed them of anything to say to each other. Iona drove swiftly, trying to marshal her thoughts about the task in front of her, still feeling shaken when she thought of Matt's body close to hers, the passion of his kiss and the fact that it was probably just part of the flirting game to him.

Matt's arms were folded over his chest, his eyes fixed straight ahead in deep thought. A jumble of emotions revolved in his mind about his feelings for Iona. She was everything he needed, wanted—but he couldn't get the past out of his head, a past that haunted him and coloured the present with feelings of remorse and guilt. He'd given in to his longing to make love to Iona, but he knew in his bones that it was too soon in their relationship for that—she had made mistakes in her love life, and so had he.

Rushing pell-mell into an affair after his experience in Africa was fraught with danger, he reflected as Iona drove through the streets of Sellingford to the scene of the accident.

CHAPTER SIX

THEY could tell where the accident was even before they got there, from the number of flashing blue lights at the top of the hill and the whine of emergency vehicle sirens as they raced to the scene.

'Looks pretty horrific,' muttered Matt grimly as he parked some way down the road to give the ambulances room to get near. 'Bet Lucas said all the necessary equipment's on board one of the ambulances, and we can pick up our suits there—so let's go!'

They both ran to the scene, skidding to a halt for a moment as the full picture hit their eyes.

'My God...' said Iona slowly. 'However did this happen?'

Under the arc lights, like some ghastly scene in a film, police and firemen were already trying to clear the road of a tangle of motorcycles which had been splayed across a corner of the country road that led to the motorway. Wheels, broken glass and belongings lay scattered over a wide area and, more obscenely, bodies lay trapped by their machines, some ominously still and quiet. One or two bikers in their leather gear wandered about the grass verge, still in their helmets, disorientated and in shock.

Although it was late at night, one or two people had gathered to watch the scene in horrified fascination and a policeman was cordoning off the area to prevent them coming too near. Matt and Iona pushed their way forward.

'We're part of the medical team here,' Matt explained, 'If you could let us through, please.'

The policeman held up a parcel for them. 'You must be Drs Carter and Bellamy—this protective gear's been left for you.'

They pulled the green suits on over their own clothes—each one had a fluorescent strip with the word DOCTOR written across the chest and back. A paramedic ran up to them immediately.

'We've got several major injuries. We've been trying to triage them, but we haven't covered everyone yet. There's at least seven we need to see.'

'What happened?' asked Matt.

'A whole group of motorcyclists were coming back from some meeting. We think the road was made slippery by all the rain and as they were cornering here someone went over, causing all this carnage.'

He pointed to a knot of firemen and medics clustered round a figure lying on the ground under not one but two bikes that had fallen on the victim.

'They're trying to lift machines from that man over there. He looks pretty bad. Could you go and assess his injuries?'

Several firemen were trying to crank up the twisted motorbikes with a heavy-duty jack, and the man's face was twisted with pain, his eyes closed.

'You'll be all right, mate,' said one of the firemen reassuringly. 'We've got the medics here, and they'll see to you when we've eased you out.'

Matt bent down and put his face near the man's. 'What's your name?' he asked.

'Grant,' whispered the man through gritted teeth. 'Please…can you do something for the pain?'

'Yes, we can. Where does it hurt?'

'My legs. They seem to be trapped—something's sticking into them.'

'I can give you something that will help,' promised Matt. He turned to the firemen. 'How long is this going to take, do you think?'

The man pulled a face. 'We've got to take it slowly. As you can see, a piece of metal's stuck into his leg. If we pull this off too quickly it could cause a lot of damage.'

Matt nodded. 'I see what you mean—we want to injure the tissues as little as possible. Could be the metal's caused a lot of damage already.'

He beckoned over one of the paramedics who had just despatched one stretcher to the first ambulance. 'Can you get a drip over here quickly, and oxygen?'

Grant gave a faint moan, and Iona took out a pre-packed syringe from the medical box. 'We're going to give you some diamorphine for the pain,' she said, turning to Matt. 'Five milligrams should help.'

'It's going to be difficult to get that needle in—he's trapped up to his neck,' said Matt grimly.

'There's a space lower down between the handle-bars—I can see his arm there. I'm smaller than you, so I could wriggle in and—'

'No way,' said Matt sharply. 'Do you want the whole thing to collapse on top of you? We'd be dealing with two casualties then! Remember, this is a team thing.'

'I can do it!' insisted Iona, already crouching down. 'Can you shine a torch into that space?' she asked one of the fireman standing by.

'Wait a minute,' said Matt roughly. 'I'm not having this, you risking your life. The whole thing could collapse.' He put his arms on her shoulders, trying to pull her away from the tangled metal.

Iona turned round at him furiously. 'Will you let me go? I can see his arm clearly now, and I can get an IV line in as well. I'm damn well going to do it, Matt, so just back off!'

Her eyes sparked across at him with a look of challenge, and for a second they glared at each other. Then he shook his head and gave an unwilling laugh.

'OK. You win! But take it slowly.' He looked down at Grant quizzically. 'Do women always fight to get near you like this?'

Grant smiled, a pale effort but definitely an attempt to be upbeat. 'You get used to it, mate,' he said hoarsely. Then he added with a brave wink, 'Most of them aren't such a knockout as this one! Save yourself for me, darlin', until I'm in one piece again!'

Iona wriggled as far as she could between the gaps in the machinery, which two fireman had covered with blankets to stop the jagged edges cutting into her. Matt handed her the IV line for the haemacel to replace the man's lost fluids and then the syringe that held the diamorphine. He kept up a steady flow of small talk to the imprisoned man, calming him, letting him know that they were doing all they could to help him.

'How's it going?' he asked tensely after what seemed endless minutes.

Iona's muffled voice came back, 'All done now. I could do with a lift as I come back through the hole.'

Immediately Matt leant forward and with powerful hands supported her weight as she pulled back, scrabbling to get some purchase. It took some time, but at last she emerged, her face covered with mud and oil, her sleeves torn. She scrambled to her feet, Matt's hands still round her waist, and looked up at him impishly.

'There you are—told you I could do it!'

He looked down at her sternly. 'Of all the stubborn women…' he said softly.

They looked at each other wryly, and Matt released his hands, suddenly feeling an entirely inappropriate urge to cuddle her close to him, feel again her sensual curves. He was shaken by the strength of his concern for her and the enormous relief he'd felt when she'd reappeared safely.

'I'm darned if I'll let you do that again,' he growled.

A hefty-looking fireman came up to them. 'Stand back, please, while we try and lift this machinery. We've cut away as much of the loose metal as we can…' He squatted by the trapped man and said in a comforting voice, 'We're going to get you out of here now, mate. Don't worry about the noise.'

A sound of creaking, grinding and scraping of metal on metal filled the air, and gradually the tangle of twisted metal was taken away from the victim. A paramedic rushed forward and a collar was put round Grant's neck before he was strapped to a spinal board, and an oxygen mask was put over his face.

'Warn the trauma unit about this man's condition,' said Matt to the paramedic as he watched Grant being stretchered over to the ambulance. 'I think we could be looking at a fractured tibia and fibia, query pelvis. We need to get the orthopaedic consultant down to see him on arrival.'

It was hard to keep calm in the mêlée of bodies and people and decide who to go to first. By a gate on the verge a man was sitting slumped against the stone wall. As Iona approached him he was struggling to take off his helmet. She moved over quickly and put a hand on his arm.

'Don't take that off until we've assessed how injured you are. You might have damaged your neck…'

'I've got to get it off,' the man muttered thickly. 'It's my throat—I've done something to it…'

Iona knelt beside him and looked as closely as she could under the rim of the helmet. She could see a deep gash in his throat, from which a thin stream of blood oozed out. Iona looked around. He'd obviously cut it in some way—but on what, and how, when the helmet had protected him?

She wondered if something on his helmet had sliced into him on impact and caused the bleed. His bike lay by his side, and it looked as if he'd hit the stone wall and been pitched forward onto the grass. Then, with a sickening feeling of horror, Iona saw a piece of wire stretched across the gateway and realised that the victim had probably sliced his neck on the wire as he'd come off the bike, and there was no way of knowing how deeply it had cut in. Until they knew the extent of his spinal and neck injuries she could not remove his helmet—it might be the only thing holding a broken neck together.

One thing she mustn't do was communicate her horror of the situation to the man in front of her. She held his hand firmly, knowing how important touch was in calming people, letting them know there was help close at hand.

'Matt,' she called, seeing he had despatched his patient in an ambulance already. 'Can you come over here?' Her voice dropped as he came towards her.

'What do we do with this man? I suspect he's got a serious injury under that helmet...I think he's practically been garotted with the wire across the gateway.'

Matt squinted as best he could under the rim of the helmet. 'His head probably came up on impact, leaving his throat vulnerable for a split second,' he said. 'The bleed doesn't seem too bad but I can't see how deep it is. Keep him as still as possible—we daren't move that helmet until he's had an X-ray, of course. All we can do at the moment is give him IV fluids and oxygen—and keep talking to him.'

Matt's voice was unflurried and authoritative as he spoke to the two paramedics who had come forward to help. A young girl suddenly appeared from nowhere, and flung herself at the side of the young man.

'Bernie,' she sobbed. 'Oh, God, I thought you'd be dead. Is he all right? Will he be OK?'

'You just leave him to us, love,' said one of the paramedics. 'You his girlfriend?'

'Yes...yes. I was on the back of his bike, but I got flung off. I've been trying to find him...'

'What about you?' asked Matt. 'Have you hurt anything?'

'I think I'm OK I just seem to have grazed my arm. I was lucky, poor Bernie took the brunt of it.'

Bernie opened his eyes and licked his dry lips. 'Hi, Kath,' he muttered. 'Can she come with me in the ambulance?'

Matt took the girl's arm and looked at it. 'She may as well come with you as she ought to be checked out as well. This graze looks very dirty—you'd better go with Bernie and have it cleaned anyway.'

'We need to transfer Bernie to a spinal board,' said

Iona, as a paramedic panted up with the required IV lines, trundling an oxygen cylinder with him.

Between them they lowered the man as gently as possible onto the board, and strapped him down rigidly to save his spine and neck from further trauma.

They watched Bernie being stretchered toward an ambulance, his girlfriend walking beside him and holding his hand. Iona sighed and passed a weary hand over her forehead.

'How many more?' she asked, looking round the devastated scene.

'I think all the majors have gone now,' said one of the paramedics. 'Just a few walking wounded left who are going to Sellingford for check-ups.'

'Then we'd better follow them,' said Matt. 'I guess they could do with our help.'

It was a long night, and all the staff were stretched to treat the victims of the two major accidents in the area. Many young people had been hurt at the disco when the building had collapsed, and there were patients lined up in the corridors on trolleys either waiting to be seen or waiting for ward beds.

Bet Lucas was magnificent, organising staff and patients like a field marshal, bullying porters to find trolleys from other departments and managing to persuade wards to relinquish their nurses to help out in Casualty.

At four o'clock in the morning Iona and several others sank onto chairs in the kitchen and Jan prepared huge mugs of coffee. Bet Lucas went to a cupboard and produced several bars of chocolate.

'Keep your blood sugar up, everyone,' she commanded. She looked down at Iona. 'What time are

you and Dr Carter back tomorrow, or rather today?'
she asked.

'In about four and a half hours,' said Iona tiredly.

'Well Mr Conlan wants you to go and get some
sleep now—he thinks the worst is over.'

Iona dragged herself up and almost banged into
Matt as she walked out of the door.

'We've got a few hours off,' she said. 'Although I
wonder if it's worth bothering to go home!'

Matt grinned. 'I doubt if you'd find a bed in this
hospital anyway at the moment!'

'Your car's at my house,' Iona said as they walked
to the car park. 'You'll need it tomorrow, won't you?'

He nodded. 'I suppose so. At the moment I don't
feel I'll ever be back in time for the day shift—I could
sleep for the week!'

'Would...would you like to stay at my house—
save you driving again?'

Iona looked up at him tentatively, feeling she ought
to make the offer—Matt looked dead on his feet—
but was unwilling to put them both in a compromising
situation again.

He gave a wry smile. 'Would you mind? I think
perhaps we'll both go out like a light—I'll just crash
out on the sofa.'

Iona awoke as the daylight streamed through the half-
open curtains into the bedroom and lay blinking lazily
as the morning sun warmed her face. In the background she could hear the sound of noises from the
kitchen, and the smell of coffee wafted tantalisingly
up the stairs. Gradually the events of the previous
evening came back to her, the horror of the road crash
almost obliterating the memory of the time leading up

to that—the delicious meal, and then the heady and passionate embraces she and Matt had exchanged. Thank God they'd both been so shattered when they'd come back from the hospital that there'd been no thought of a goodnight kiss—just a total collapse onto the sofa and the bed!

She rolled over with a sigh. Things had gone rather fast last night and she had never meant to get so heavy with Matt. He might look at their kisses as a pleasant diversion, but she could never regard them so lightly. In the cold light of day she wondered why on earth she'd responded so eagerly. She had to work with this man, for heaven's sake, and it would get more and more difficult to maintain a professional relationship if making love to him was all she could think about!

Iona tensed as she heard a gentle knock on her bedroom door, and pulled the sheet hurriedly up to her neck. From now on, she vowed, she had to cool it with Matt—friendly, yes, professional, yes, but too loving—no!

'Come in,' she said briskly.

Matt appeared with a steaming cup of coffee and some buttered toast. 'Here you are, madam,' he said gravely. 'You've got ten minutes to have this and be ready for work!'

She stared at him, and then gave a little shriek. 'What's the time?' She sat bolt upright, so that the sheet slid down from her body and revealed the skimpy nightdress she'd flung on the night before, and looked at her bedside clock. 'Oh, my God—it's eight o'clock. I'll never make it!'

She grabbed a hand mirror by the bed and squinted into it, giving another cry of despair. 'I look terrible.

I need to wash my hair—I can't go to work looking like this!'

Matt set the tray down by the side of her bed, his eyes sweeping over her disordered hair tumbling over her shoulders and eyes still a little heavy with sleep. His gaze held something more than admiration in them, and his lips twitched in a little smile.

'You look fine to me. Perhaps the nightie's a little brief for a ward round—but I wouldn't worry about your hair at all! In fact,' he added, after a brief pause, 'you look pretty damn good to me!'

Iona pulled the sheet back up to her chin. 'I don't believe a word of what you say—but, please, go out while I make myself decent for work!' A slightly embarrassed expression crossed her face. 'By the way…it was a lovely meal last night. Thank you very much.'

He looked at her quizzically. 'I enjoyed it, too. We got to know each other quite well, didn't we?'

Iona reddened slightly and looked at him under her lashes. 'Look, this is awkward…but I felt I might have given you the wrong impression last night. I was a little enthusiastic perhaps.'

'You enjoyed yourself!' he corrected her. 'Nothing wrong in that, is there?'

'No. I just wouldn't want you to get the wrong idea. I mean, I want us to be friends but…'

'But you don't want to take things too fast?' he finished for her with a grin. 'Make haste slowly, my old grannie used to say.'

He stepped forward and lifted her face with his finger under her chin, holding her gaze with dancing grey eyes. 'Yes, I want to be friends with you as well,' he said softly, adding with smiling emphasis, 'Quite intimate friends, in fact!'

Iona opened her mouth in faint protest. 'I didn't mean that.'

Matt put a finger over her lips. 'It's all right—I know what you mean. You don't want to make a mistake again—is that right?'

Something like that, thought Iona wryly. Neither do I want to be just a passing fancy for Matt Carter!

He flicked a look at his watch and grimaced. 'I'll get going now—one of us ought to be on time! Meanwhile, don't forget you promised to come to my father's farewell do next week. Although I think we should see each other before that—cement our friendship, you might say!'

With a cheeky grin and a wink he disappeared, and she heard his footsteps clattering down the stairs and the bang of the front door as he left the house.

Oh, hell, thought Iona tremulously, it's going to be very very difficult to stop myself falling for Matt this time!

Despite her misgivings about her feelings for Matt, Iona felt an unreasonable happiness and lightness of heart at work. The fact that Bet Lucas was in an even sharper mood than usual, lecturing everyone about oxygen cylinders which had been left in front of exit doors and the state of the cups in the kitchen, didn't dampen her spirits at all.

'You look pretty happy,' whispered Chloe as they passed each other in the corridor. 'Go well last night, did it?'

'Do you mean the red alert at the hospital?' asked Iona innocently. 'That was a bit hairy actually!'

'I didn't mean that, you donkey! What about earlier on in the evening—was there a red alert between you and Matt?'

'We had a very nice time,' stated Iona primly. 'I can recommend the food at that pub!'

Chloe looked at her in exasperation. 'You, Iona Bellamy, are the most irritating woman in this entire hospital. I want to know all about Matt "Superman" Carter, not what flaming food you ate! I'll see you later!'

She scurried off, and Iona gave an inward chuckle. Chloe wouldn't rest until she'd wormed out the extent of Matt's relationship with her, and as she walked towards the cubicle to see her next patient, Iona wondered dreamily if she knew herself!

Jan was standing taking deep breaths outside the cubicle as Iona came up. She smiled ruefully at Iona.

'Just getting some fresh air! It's a little close in there—we've got an old friend visiting us. I have sprayed the air surreptitiously, but my oxygen level's taken a dive!'

Iona raised her eyebrows and grinned. 'Don't say it's Maisie Butler again...she was only here a few days ago. What's wrong this time?'

Maisie Butler was well known to the unit. She wandered into the department on a regular basis—a large, untidy woman with an ancient coat tied round the middle with string, carrying numerous bags and bulging plastic parcels. Her swollen feet were pushed into old slippers, and her rough hands had half-fingered woollen mittens on them, even now, when it was summer.

Maisie used the hospital as an occasional refuge when life got too lonely and she needed people around her. Usually the staff would turn a blind eye when she sat in the casualty waiting room because they were fond of her, and as long as she didn't disrupt things, she did little harm. She was part of the mosaic of humanity that came through Casualty's doors, a poor old lady who needed occasional company and cosseting.

Iona pushed the curtains apart. Maisie was lying propped up on the bed, lank-haired and flushed, with all her parcels and bags surrounding her.

'Hello, Maisie, what's the matter? We only saw you last week…you said you felt fine then.'

Maisie looked at her lugubriously. 'I had a funny turn in the shopping centre—felt dizzy and sick. They wanted to get an ambulance, but I don't like them— they go too fast. Made my own way here.'

'You should have let them bring you—saved your poor old feet,' said Iona, taking out her stethoscope and putting the trumpet end on Maisie's chest. 'Have you felt like this before?'

'Had a few turns lately…old age, I guess.' Maisie gave a cackle of laughter and then subsided back with a paroxysm of coughing.

'How long have you had this cough?'

'For a while—don't usually get it until the winter. It's come on a bit sudden this year. Hurts my chest, it does, when I start.'

Iona looked at her assessingly. 'You've lost a bit of weight, Maisie…what's your appetite like?'

Maisie pulled a face. 'Don't fancy much these days. I cough up this phlegm and it puts you off food.'

'I think you've got a bit of a fever,' commented Iona, stuffing her stethoscope back in her pocket. 'I'd like you to have an X-ray, although you may have to wait for a while.'

A smile spread over Maisie's tired old face. 'That's all right, love, I don't mind waiting. What about a cup of tea? I could do with something hot and sweet and then I'll have a little nap until they're ready to get me!'

Iona smiled as she went to get a cup of tea from the machine for Maisie—it was nice for the poor old thing to have a bit of spoiling!

Waiting by the drinks machine was Matt, pushing coins into the slot and then banging it irritably.

'This thing has some terminal disease,' he muttered, turning round when he saw Iona. 'It keeps shooting out the wrong stuff.'

'I thought you only liked freshly ground coffee,' Iona teased.

'It's not coffee I want—it's that thick slab of chocolate stuffed with nuts, just looking at me provocatively, that I crave,' he said ruefully. 'Then I can eat it with my freshly ground coffee!'

'Well, I'm getting a cup of tea for Maisie,' Iona said, pushing the button choice.

'Who's Maisie?'

Iona laughed. 'She's one of our regulars—you've probably missed her. Usually she doesn't have anything much wrong with her that a bath and a proper diet wouldn't help. Just likes to pop into Casualty for a bit of company, I think.'

'Ah, a bit of a loner, is she?'

'I don't think Maisie has a fixed address—probably shop doorways and railway arches are her home I'm afraid—but I think that's the way she wants to live most of the time.' Iona wrinkled her brow. 'She's not well at the moment, though. I'm sending her for a chest X-ray—she's rattling away like an express engine, her temperature's up and she says she's coughing up phlegm. I wouldn't mind your opinion, Matt.'

Maisie looked up coquettishly at Matt as he came in. 'My, oh, my! I didn't know I was going to see Dr Irresistible! I'd have put my best bib and tucker on if I known you'd be looking at me!'

He grinned back at her. 'Bet you say that to all the men,' he teased. 'I'm Dr Carter and Dr Bellamy's just asked me to have a look at you.'

Maisie's eyes flicked from Matt to Iona and chuckled. 'I must have the two best-looking doctors in the hospital. You make a very handsome couple—are you courting?'

'Mind your own business, Maisie,' retorted Iona primly. 'We just work together, that's all!'

Maisie took no notice. 'If I were you, young man, I'd grab Dr Bellamy before someone else does! You don't see hair that colour every day—it shows a fiery character, that does!'

He raised quizzical eyebrows at her. 'That's probably very good advice—and I agree with you about the hair!' He flicked laughing eyes over to Iona then turned back to his patient. 'And now I'd like to ask you some questions. I believe you've got a bad cough—ever coughed up any blood?'

'Oh, yes, the place where I sleep, most of us do that!'

'And where do you sleep, Maisie?' asked Matt gently.

'Depends. In the summer it's usually the rain shelter in the park—or a bench. But I don't mind that—means I'm fancy-free,' she said rather defiantly.

'You must get a bit cold and wet—especially on a night like last night,' Matt observed. 'Lean forward and let me just tap your back with my fingers.'

He leant forward to listen to the resonance of sound he produced, and Iona stood back watching him, her arms folded, trying to concentrate on his percussion of Maisie's chest rather than how she would love to run her fingers through the dark hair that curled slightly on the back of his neck and the unnerving sight of his strong profile and the firm lips that had been pressed to hers so ardently the night before.

She pulled herself back to the present as Matt patted Maisie's hand reassuringly. 'Now, you just relax back and have the tea Dr Bellamy's got you. We'll be back soon.'

Both doctors went out of the cubicle and Iona looked up at Matt enquiringly. 'Is it what I think it could be?' she asked.

'If you're thinking of tuberculosis, I'd bet on it,' he answered wryly. 'There's a lot of indicators pointing in that direction. She sounds like she has a pneumothorax. After her X-rays we'd better run a tuberculin and sputum test—and do her bloods.'

'Poor old Maisie,' sighed Iona. 'I'd better tell her she'll be in longer than it takes to drink a cup of tea. We ought to keep her in for a few days.'

She smiled brightly at the old lady as they went back into the cubicle. 'We'd like to do a few tests on you, Maisie,' she began.

'Am I dying? What do you think's up with me?' Maisie voice was perky. In the secure environment of the hospital she obviously felt quite happy.

Iona hesitated, unwilling to say what she thought until they had a definite result. 'I'm sure that you'll be fine, but we want to make sure,' she said cautiously. 'That's why we're trying to find a bed for you—the results of these tests can take a few days to come through.'

'I'll have to stay in, then?'

'Hopefully not for too long.'

Maisie leant back on the pillows and sighed with contentment. 'D'you know, I was feeling so tired recently and I need a holiday—is breakfast and dinner included?'

'I think you're just faking this to get board and lodging,' teased Matt. 'Tell me, Maisie, have you any relatives? Surely someone would want to know that you're not very well and come and see you?'

Maisie compressed her lips together. 'No one I'd want to see,' she growled, but an expression of sadness flickered momentarily across her face.

'Are you sure?' persisted Iona, watching her carefully. 'We could get in touch with them.'

Maisie looked down at the sheet and said nothing for a while, then looked up at Iona, her eyes glistening with tears. 'You're very kind, Doctor,' she whispered. 'There is someone I'd really like to see before I die…'

'You aren't going to die yet, Maisie,' said Matt sternly. 'Put that out of your head. Now, who is this someone?'

'It's my daughter—I haven't seen her for ever so long. I'd like to see her again—in here, where I'm clean and in nice surroundings…'

Iona felt a lump in her own throat—nobody probably thought that Maisie was aware of her own grubby appearance, or minded about where she lived. She patted the old lady's hand and smiled very kindly at her. 'That's a wonderful idea, Maisie. We'll get in touch with her—it will be something for you to look forward to.'

'She's the only person I know who positively welcomes coming into hospital,' said Iona to Matt later when Maisie had been taken to an isolation ward pending the results of her tests. 'She'll probably go out much improved after regular food.'

'And come back a few weeks later to square one! Pity she can't be found some accommodation. It makes you wonder what the story is that brought her to this state, doesn't it?'

They were taking up one of the bulging parcels Maisie had left behind her in the cubicle and to give her some good news. When they arrived at Maisie's bed, they found she had emptied one of her bags and was examining the contents which were spread over the bed, together with a tray of food.

Maisie looked up happily. 'Eh, they're good to me in here. I've had the best tea I've had in years!'

'The management will be glad to hear that—a champion of hospital food!' remarked Iona, laughing. 'We've got a message for you—we contacted the number you gave me, and your daughter's coming in tomorrow. She sounded very excited!'

Maisie sighed. 'I don't know if I've done the right thing—it's been a few years now. We had a falling out and she didn't seem to want to know me...'

She scrabbled around in the possessions on the bed and pounced on something, holding it up to show them. It was a photograph of a young woman holding a pretty little girl by the hand, and both of them were laughing into the camera. The young woman was slender and incredibly beautiful, with blonde hair piled on the top of her head and wearing a dress that revealed long, tanned legs. Iona took it and looked at it carefully.

'That's a lovely photograph,' she said, 'Who is it?'

'That was me and my daughter,' Maisie said. 'Hard to believe, isn't it? The years roll by and you think everything will stay the same—but it doesn't.' She put a handkerchief to her nose and blew it. 'I never thought I'd end up like this. I just wish I looked a bit better when Patsy comes to see me.'

'I think she'll be so glad to know where you are and see you again. She won't mind what you look like,' said Matt softly.

They walked down the corridor together, sombre for a minute as they reflected on the sad story of Maisie.

'I can't believe that photo was the same woman in the bed now,' said Iona, 'What an incredible story she must have to tell…'

'I guess that most of us have a secret agenda that's coloured what we are today,' answered Matt, his voice bleak. 'Things in our lives that we'd rather no one knew about.'

Iona looked at him sharply. She'd caught that note of despondency before, and she noticed how a muscle worked in his face as if he was trying to suppress his feelings. She guessed whatever it was that Matt hid from the public was never very far from the surface.

'Is…is there anything the matter?' she asked tentatively, unwilling to appear too prying.

He gave the ghost of a smile before straightening his shoulders. 'No—I can't change the past,' he said quietly, then warm grey eyes looked down at her, holding her gaze in his. 'And I'm beginning to think the future holds much more promise than I ever could have believed!'

He put an arm round her shoulders and briefly squeezed her affectionately, and a dart of pleasure winged through Iona. Perhaps Matt really did like her for herself and not just as another conquest. He was right about the future, she decided happily, it really *did* hold promise!

CHAPTER SEVEN

THE swimming pool was steamy and noisy and about the last place she wanted to be after a hard day's work, thought Iona. She and Jan stood at the side of the pool, towelling their hair dry after spending half an hour in the municipal baths as part of their training for the sponsored swim organised by the 'Friends' of the hospital to raise funds for a new scanner.

'I didn't realise how unfit I was,' Iona admitted. 'Trying to plough up and down through hordes of school kids has left me whacked! I'll have to work at it if I'm to do this sponsored swim—I feel as if I've swum the Channel instead of eight feeble lengths!'

'At least you don't need to lose any weight—I've got to lose ten pounds!' Jan looked mournfully at Iona. 'It'll be crispbreads and low-cal fish meals for ages, and not a vestige of chocolate!'

'What's brought all this on? Are you going on holiday?'

'No such luck. It's just that I said to this really obese patient who came in yesterday that if I could lose weight, so could he—so he's coming back in three weeks and we're going to compare notes! I shall feel such a fool if I end up gaining weight, like I did on my last diet!'

Iona grinned. 'You'll be like a pencil if we keep up this exercise every day—everyone in the unit's pledged to get into shape before the big swim.'

'You're right about everyone getting into training,'

said Jan, nodding at the doorway. 'Look who's here—it's only Magnificent Matt! I'm going before he sees me looking like a whale in this costume. I'll see you later!'

She bolted for the changing rooms and with a shiver of excitement Iona watched Matt go to the deep end and execute a perfect running dive. The brief glance she had of a tanned, lean torso and muscular legs was enough to make her heart thump and her legs feel rather like melting jelly. The whole week had been like that—whenever he'd been near her at work, she'd had this incredible heightened awareness, every nerve in her body tingling and a longing to be in his arms once more.

It wasn't her imagination—but she was sure he felt very much the same way. Why else would he hold her hand a fraction longer than necessary when passing her something, or put his arm round her shoulders when showing her a report? And why insist that he should come round tonight when her nephews were staying at her place for the night while their parents were out?

'A penny for them?'

His deep voice sounded in her ear, and Iona jumped out of her reverie. Matt was standing next to her, exuding latent power and making every other man standing round the pool look rather weedy and pale. He swept a slow, intimate look over her, taking in her soft curves and creamy skin, accentuated by her clinging pale blue swimsuit, and his eyes danced at her.

'Someone told me the local baths were dreary—how wrong they were!'

Iona laughed. 'I take it that's a compliment? Don't ask me about my swimming, though!'

'So how many lengths have you swum?' he asked.

'Not many—I won't be much good for the sponsored swim,' she admitted. 'I've got to try and get into shape.'

He gave a low chuckle. 'I'd have thought you didn't have to worry on that score! Did I see you with Jan Fielding?'

'Yes—she and I are trying to get fit together.'

'I think she'll have to work harder at it than you will,' he observed cheekily. 'Now, what time shall I come tonight?'

Iona thought of her brother's and sister-in-law's intense interest in her love life and sighed. 'Perhaps it would be better if you didn't come,' she said feebly, knowing only too well that she wanted nothing more than for him to be near her!

'Why not?' he looked at her, as if astonished. 'Surely Pete and Mary would be pleased you had a friend round?'

'Well, if they saw you when they brought the children round, they might think er...well, that we were an item, or something ridiculous like that!'

Matt's eyes darkened as he looked at her. 'Iona, sweetheart, let them think what they like—you're a big girl now!' He grinned impishly. 'Besides, I very much want to help you with the paper you're writing on child care in Casualty—that will be the major part of my agenda! What time are they bringing the boys?'

'About seven. They're going to some reception in London, so won't be back until tomorrow.'

'Excellent! Then I'll come to your place at about seven-thirty with some wine and food, and we'll do an in-depth study on what to put in your paper!'

Iona gave a nervous giggle. She couldn't imagine

being able to concentrate on anything at all academic if Matt was around—and just what did he mean by his 'agenda'?

'I can do the paper myself, you know…and it'll be very boring just sitting with the boys while they're asleep.'

He looked at her enigmatically. 'You think? I have a feeling we won't be bored at all…' He bent down and brushed her mouth with his, and his lips were warm and firm. 'I'm looking forward to it,' he whispered, then turned and plunged back into the pool.

Iona touched her tingling lips with her finger, and watched him ploughing up and down the water, muscular arms powering him along. In the last week a new understanding seemed to have grown up between them—intense awareness and a kind of elation in each other's company. She didn't really know why, but a suppressed feeling of excitement filled her when she thought about the coming evening—a sense that tonight would be some kind of watershed in their relationship.

Sam, Jack and Freddy had gone upstairs, and Iona could hear their raucous shouts and laughter as they played a new computer game she'd bought them. She had promised they could play for half an hour before they went to bed, and when she'd informed them that Matt would be coming to keep her company that evening they had demanded that he come up to play it with them.

'What are you going to do this evening, Iona?' Freddy, the youngest, had asked.

'I'm writing an article for a magazine about how

we look after children in Casualty,' said Iona virtuously.

'And Matt's going to help you, is he?'

'Er, yes, that's right!'

The sound of a car coming up the drive sent the little boys careering to the front door and flinging it open.

'Wow, Matt, that's a fantastic car you've got there! Is it new?'

Iona followed them to the door, and was surprised to see a bright red, new-looking and very snazzy sports car parked in front of the house. Matt smiled at the four impressed faces.

'It's new to me,' he informed them. 'I decided my old car had come to the end of the line, so I've got into even more debt by buying this little beauty!' He looked mischievously at Iona. 'I hope you won't get quite so wet in this one if it rains!'

Having admired the car, the boys went off to bed after Matt had beaten them all at the computer game. When the children were sound asleep, he and Iona sat outside drinking wine in the little private rose garden to the side of the house where the smell of honeysuckle and sweet lavender filtered over to them in the soft night air. Through an arch in the protective hedge they could see the lawn which was already filled with the paraphernalia the boys had left there—an old football, a skateboard and a mini-scooter slung against the tree.

'They're lucky children to have you,' Matt remarked. 'Lots of room to play—and they've got each other to play with.'

'Have you any brothers and sisters?' asked Iona, curious to know more about Matt's life.

'Unfortunately, no. It's hard sometimes, being an only child—it can be difficult to live up to the high expectations of your parents.'

'They must be very proud of you…'

Matt shrugged and pulled a wry face. 'My father's something of a perfectionist—in work and life generally. Some of his hopes for me haven't been fulfilled—and he likes reminding me of them!'

'He sounds a bit fierce.' Iona laughed. 'I'll be frightened of meeting him at his retirement party!'

'Oh, don't worry—he can be very charming. And I know he'll love you—how could he not?' Matt's eyes softened, and he ran a finger gently through Iona's tumbling hair, trailing it down her neck to the V in her cleavage. 'I'll probably have a hard time keeping you to myself that night!' he whispered.

He turned her face to his, and for an instant their eyes locked, but she was the first to lower hers, almost embarrassed by the passion she saw there. He took her hand in his and pressed it to his lips, nibbling little kisses on her fingers. Iona's heartbeat bounded into overdrive in response to his touch, but she didn't pull her hand away, just sat very still, every nerve tingling in anticipation of what she knew he would do.

She made a feeble attempt to put the brakes on their mounting physical attraction. 'We shouldn't get too heavy…the boys might hear us,' she gulped.

'Of course we shouldn't,' he said smoothly, wicked laughter dancing in his eyes. 'We'll be very circumspect.'

Then he stood up and pulled her from her chair, his gaze burning into her face, feasting on the softness of her skin, the sweep of her eyelashes over her cheeks. He drew her closely towards him so that they were standing breast to breast, hip to hip—so close she could smell the tang of his aftershave, feel his warm breath on her cheek. His arms went round her waist and he pulled her into an embrace so hard against him that she could feel the taut wall of his stomach muscles against the softness of her body.

'Oh, God, it's impossible to sit next to you all night and not do this,' he said huskily. 'You are so beautiful…'

Iona felt the blood pound in her ears, and her heart clattered uncomfortably against her ribs at the suddenness of it all. She barely knew what she was saying. 'Aren't you hungry?' she said breathlessly. 'What about all the food you've brought?'

'Yes, too right I'm hungry, Iona—but not for food, I've lost my appetite. It's you I want you so much.'

'Matt,' she protested, trying not to giggle, 'Remember, the children are upstairs…'

He grinned down at her, his eyes twinkling. 'So? We're down here. They won't know, and we can hear them if they need us.'

It was a beautiful night—still balmy, with a velvety sky punctuated with brilliant stars and the silver sickle of a moon rising above the rooftop. Iona stretched contentedly against him, luxuriating in the feel of his hard body on hers, knowing that everything was right—the surroundings, the soft romantic evening and, most of all, Matt so close to her.

He looked down at her tenderly. 'Happy?' he asked softly, and she nodded wordlessly, turning her face up to his.

He lifted her thick hair back from her neck, and then with passionate intensity his mouth bruised hers in fierce kisses, moving down her jawline, her neck, and her breasts, through the thin material of her cotton shirt. Iona couldn't help herself—she leaned into him heavily, loving the sensation of his hard mouth on her soft skin, returning his kisses just as passionately. His impetuousness gave her no time for rational consideration, and when he pulled her gently to the ground, she didn't resist him.

The grass was soft, and a fresh earthy smell of a dew-dampened garden enveloped them. Iona stretched out luxuriously, basking in the feel of his hands caressing her and his tongue fluttering over her body so that her back arched in pleasure against his hard body. He started to unbutton her shirt, and gently pulled down her short skirt so that she felt the sweetness of their naked skin against each other and the hardness of his desire. Her hands roamed over his chest and back, revelling in the satiny feel of his firm muscles and her ability to make him groan with pleasure.

He looked down at her lovingly. 'Is this what you want, my darling? I only want to make love to you if you want it, too…'

It was too late to draw back, and neither did she want to. Wasn't this what she'd really longed for and dreamed about for three years, ever since he'd taken her to the dance, and even later when she'd been engaged to Kevin? Suddenly she felt a sense of release, as if she had managed to let the past go. From now on she was going to turn her attention to the future—forget and forgive herself about the mistakes she'd made.

For answer she wound her arms about his neck and

pulled him down on top of her. 'Yes,' she whispered. 'This is what I want, Matt…'

Then they lost themselves in each other, their limbs entwined, her silken skin against his gentle but demanding body, revelling in the waves of sweetness that flooded through her and the power she had to make Matt's body shudder with rapture. Afterwards they lay back, sated with passion, and Iona realised she had never felt so happy, so content. She twined her arms around him and looked deep into his eyes, and he smiled back lovingly, stroking back strands of her hair from her forehead.

'Could anything have been more wonderful than that, my sweet?' he said softly.

She laughed throatily. 'Is that what you call being circumspect?' she teased.

He curled round her protectively, and Iona looked up at the velvety sky, sparkling with bright stars, and a little voice whispered in her head, He must love me after that…nothing can go wrong now, can it? There can be no turning back!

Jan was writing something down very carefully on a piece of paper stuck to one of the cupboard doors in the little kitchen, having first checked something in a little book in her hand.

'What are you doing?' asked Iona curiously, as she sipped a restoring cup of coffee near the end of a hectic morning.

'Calorie-counting,' said Jan gloomily. 'I've had nearly half of my day's quota already, and it's not lunchtime yet!'

'God, I'd better join you if you're dieting,' said Chloe, coming into the room. 'You know that dress you lent me a few weeks ago, Iona? I can't get into at *all* now! I've brought it back for you—perhaps you want to wear it tonight at the Prof's farewell bash.' She looked impishly at Iona. 'I take it you *are* going with Dr You Know Who!'

'I might be.' Iona's eyes danced across the room at them, but she said primly, 'You are the nosiest lot. I happen to be a long-standing friend of Matt's, you know—so, of course, he'd like me to be along…'

The other two grinned knowingly and winked at each other. 'Of course he would!' they chorused. 'So what *are* you going to wear? It'll be a pretty posh do—isn't it at the Prof's gorgeous mansion?'

'I don't know what to wear. I might splash out on something new—I'm off this afternoon,' admitted Iona, butterflies of excitement already fluttering inside her.

Every night for a week, since that wonderful night she and Matt had made love, they had been together, unable to have enough of each other. She was living on cloud nine, euphoric with happiness. There was only the slightest shadow on the horizon, but barely a trace of concern—Matt had not yet said he loved her. But it would happen, Iona thought happily. Of course he loved her—he was mad about her!

The door was pushed open and Bet Lucas came bustling in, exuding an air of efficiency.

'Ah, here you are, Dr Bellamy. Could you come and look at a patient in cubicle four?' Her face took on a slightly mysterious expression, and her voice sank to a whisper as if there might be bugging devices hidden around.

'Absolute discretion here. The gentleman happens to be in the public eye, and although I know we are discreet with all our patients, of course, he is particularly keen that the press or any media should not know that he or his companion are here. It could be most embarrassing for him if it was common knowledge!'

The three girls looked at each other with raised eyebrows, and Iona followed Bet down to the cubicle bays. Her mind seethed with curiosity as she pushed open the curtains and then tried to suppress her expression of astonishment at seeing Lawson Barrington, the local Member of Parliament and an eminent member of the Cabinet, lying on the bed with two black eyes and pressing a pad to a wound in his neck. Whoever said hospital medicine was dull?

Standing by the bed, weeping uncontrollably and twisting a handkerchief in her hands, was a glamorous young woman—and it wasn't his wife.

'I'm sorry, I didn't want this to happen...' she sobbed. 'God, what has he done to you, Lawson?'

'Could I just see your wound?' Iona said quietly, noting the man's shocked and pale appearance and the slow oozing of the blood.

She pushed gently past the crying girl and, pulling away the gauze pad, looked carefully at the injury. Then she put a cuff round the man's arm to register his blood pressure. 'How did this happen?' she asked.

'It was my fault,' said the girl. 'My...my husband got to know about Lawson and—'

'Blanche, you little idiot—be careful what you say.' Lawson Barrington's voice was surprisingly strong and harsh. 'Do you want the whole world to know?'

The girl broke into a fresh paroxysm of crying. 'I

didn't know he knew about us, or that he'd come round and do this to you...'

'It looks like a knife wound, fortunately not very deep and quite cleanly cut,' commented Iona quickly, trying to block Blanche's mounting hysteria. 'You were attacked, then?'

The man grunted. 'He came at me like a madman with the kitchen knife...he nearly killed me!'

'You're very lucky. It appears to have just missed your windpipe—but it needs thorough cleansing and stitching to bring the perimeters of skin together, then it should heal without trouble. Have you had a recent tetanus injection?'

'Yes, yes,' said Lawson Barrington impatiently. 'A year or two ago when I went on a fact-finding mission abroad. How long will all this cleaning and stitching take? I have to get home.'

'I'll come back with you,' said Blanche tearfully. 'See you're all right...'

He groaned. 'Don't be ridiculous, Blanche. I know you mean it kindly, but my wife could come back any time. I've got to do damage limitation here. You go back to your husband like a good girl and try and placate him—say you were just doing some overtime or something.'

'But look at the wound...it's terrible. You can't go back to an empty house!' whispered the girl, gazing with horrified eyes at the cut in his neck.

'It looks worse than it is,' Iona said kindly. 'Why don't you just go and sit in the waiting room for a few minutes—get yourself a coffee from the machine? The police will want to ask Mr Barrington some questions.'

'Have we got to drag them into it? For heaven's

sake, this is a private matter…nothing to do with anyone else.' Lawson Barrington struggled to sit up. 'It was just a domestic—'

'Someone reported the disturbance, Mr Barrington, and they appear to know you've been wounded. Remember, this wound could have had very serious consequences and they're keen to know what happened.'

Blanche stumbled out of the cubicle with a hiccuping sob, and the MP sighed.

'Stupid girl,' he muttered. 'I knew she couldn't keep things to herself—probably told one of her girl friends about our little, er, liaison, and before you know it, the bloody husband's on the warpath and the police have been brought into it!'

'Really?' said Iona coldly, noticing that he attributed no guilt at all to himself. 'I'll put this pad over the wound to protect it after I've put in a few sutures. I'm sure you don't feel like moving your head too much anyway, but keep it as still as possible.'

'You're not putting that great thing on?' asked the man in dismay. 'I've got to give an address in the Commons tomorrow, which, of course, will be televised. What will everyone make of that?'

'Perhaps you could wear a scarf over it, Mr Barrington.'

He looked at her scornfully. 'In the middle of a heat wave? Don't be daft.' He stared gloomily down the bed. 'I'm ruined. Damn career's gone for a burton, I should think—and all because of a maniac!'

Iona finished suturing the wound and pulled off her latex gloves. 'There you are! Come back in a few days and we'll look at how it's healing.'

'Good! Then I can go now?'

'Certainly—after you've seen the police. I'll ask them to come in, shall I?'

Lawson Barrington sighed heavily. 'I suppose so—though I might as well put the headlines in the paper myself, CABINET MINISTER STABBED BY JEALOUS HUSBAND!' He looked defensively at Iona. 'I'm not as wicked as you think. Blanche was in financial trouble and I gave her money. We got rather fond of each other—'

'That's all right, sir,' said Iona briskly. 'It's really none of my business!'

She swept out of the cubicle and motioned to the waiting police officer to go in. Casualty certainly threw up unexpected situations, she reflected wryly. If she hadn't seen Lawson Barrington here as a patient, she might still have gone on thinking he was the perfect example of a married man, with a lovely wife and three children—for that was the image he always presented to the public!

She looked at her watch. Thank heavens it was nearly lunchtime. It had been a fiendishly busy morning with a seemingly unending procession of broken limbs, a child with an asthmatic attack and a perforated ulcer. She couldn't wait to have some time to herself and get ready for Prof Carter's party that evening!

Iona looked at herself critically in the mirror—was the slinky ice-blue number she'd fallen for that afternoon slightly too formal? It fitted her like a second skin, off the shoulder and following every curve on her body. It had been outrageously expensive, but she knew the colour suited her so much, a wonderful foil to her amber hair, and in her present euphoric mood

for once she hadn't given a thought to her bank
balance!

She sat down in front of her dressing-table and
brushed her hair, catching each side in a silver clip
and letting the rest hang freely down her back. A hint
of shadow over her eyelids, the faintest application of
blusher on her cheeks and a delicate lipstick on her
lips finished her make-up. She looked at the face that
gazed back at her from the mirror—hazel eyes large
with excitement, cheeks slightly flushed. It was the
first really public date that she and Matt had been on,
and it felt almost like some sort of debut. After tonight, everyone would know that Iona Bellamy and
Matt Carter were an item!

Matt placed a protective arm around Iona's shoulder
as they entered the vast hall of Cottesmore Manor,
his parents' home. The whole place was swirling with
people, the men in dinner jackets, the women in every
kind of dress, from short cocktail dress to voluminous
ballgown. Many of the crowd Iona recognised from
the hospital mingling with the great and the good
from every department of the local health authority.

She looked up in awe at the wonderful wide staircase that swept down to the ground from either side
of a gallery, and the intricately patterned plaster ceiling with a spectacular crystal chandelier hanging from
it. In every corner huge vases of summer flowers had
been arranged, and the air was heavy with the scent
of night stock and sweet peas. It was all magnificent
and rather daunting to think that all this belonged to
Matt's parents.

Professor and Mrs. Carter stood at the entrance to
the drawing room, from where strains of a piano fil-

tered through. They made a very handsome couple—
the Professor an older, white-haired version of his
son, tall and solid, his wife much smaller but very
pretty. Matt led Iona up to them and started the
introductions.

'Father, Mother—this is Iona Bellamy, a colleague
of mine in A and E. Iona—my parents, Tarquin and
Margaret Carter.'

They both smiled broadly at Iona, a distinct look
of approval in their eyes as they swept assessing
glances over her.

'So you've got to know Matt since he's come back,
have you?' asked Mrs. Carter chattily, obviously trying to do some unobtrusive digging about Iona!

'Actually, we knew each other before he went to
Africa,' said Iona. 'We worked for a while together
in Orthopaedics at St Olaf's.'

'Really?' His parents flashed a look at each other.
'We never heard him mention your name—although
I can't think why he should keep it a secret! He's a
real dark horse about his private life!' Mrs. Carter
gave an indulgent laugh. 'His father has to prise everything out of him!'

'You must be very pleased Matt's come back to
Sellingford,' said Iona politely.

'We certainly are! Can't think why he went in the
first place—or what made him return!'

Iona flicked a look up at Matt. His expression was
bland, but a steely look in his eyes belied a certain
sensitivity. He took her hand and squeezed it. 'I'll
take Iona off to our table—get some dancing in,' he
said firmly. 'See you later, Mother, Father.'

'You do that,' boomed Professor Carter, patting
Iona on the shoulder. 'I'm very glad to meet you, my

dear—makes me even sorrier that I'm retiring when I see what talent we have coming up!'

As Matt and Iona drifted into the large drawing room, filled with flower-decorated tables, Iona heard Professor Carter whisper to his wife, 'She'll do—she's a cracker!'

Matt grinned down at her. 'Did you hear that? You've passed a monumental test!'

Iona giggled. 'I was pretty terrified about meeting them—but they seem really nice!'

Matt led her to their table, set for ten people. 'Just leave your bag here. We'll go and have a glass of something to get us in the mood and then I want to dance with you—and only you!'

It was as if time had reversed itself and they were back at the dance three years ago—only this time Iona was sure of Matt's feelings. She only had to look up into his eyes, dark with desire as he held her close to him on the dance floor, twinkling with mischief when he twirled her round and then gathering her to him in an embrace that left her breathless and her heart pounding. Sometimes Iona was conscious of Professor Carter watching them from the side of the floor and felt slightly embarrassed—but then she thought, if Matt's laid back about his father seeing them together, why should she worry?

By the time of the dinner Iona felt heady with the champagne she and Matt had been drinking, and every nerve ending was pulsing with happiness and excitement. He led her back to the table where several people were already seated, and Iona noted with wry interest that the place setting next to hers was being removed—it had the name THE HON. LAWSON BARRINGTON, MP written on the card. She guessed that the reason given for the member of parliament's absence would be a sudden indisposition!

A tall, bespectacled man rose from his chair and said, gesturing to the empty space, 'Apparently our local MP can't make it tonight—he's indisposed.' The man smiled at them, holding out his hand to Matt. 'Can I introduce myself?' he said pleasantly, 'I'm Terry Cummings, the new hospital manager. I believe you're the Professor's son?'

'That's right—pleased to meet you. You're rather being flung in at the deep end at a gathering like this, aren't you?' Matt turned to Iona and drew her forward. 'This is Iona Bellamy, a colleague of mine in A and E.'

Terry Cummings gave Iona a warm smile and grasped her hand, a frank look of admiration in his eyes. 'Ah—I shall be visiting that department tomorrow. It's going to take time, but I'm determined to introduce myself to everyone I can in the next few days. I really want to get to know people properly...want them to feel they can unload their worries and concerns.'

'That's a good start,' said Iona, laughing, 'You may feel you're overwhelmed!'

They all sat down and started their first course of asparagus mousse—so light it melted in their mouths. Terry seemed an easy man to talk to, with plenty of anecdotes about his previous job and interested in what Matt, Iona and the other guests had to say.

'Do you know this area?' asked Matt.

Terry shook his head. 'No, but I can't wait to explore it with my children. We're all keen cyclists and I think there are plenty of places to go to round here.'

'So your wife cycles, too?'

Terry's smile faded and he said sadly, 'I'm afraid I'm a widower—my wife died a few years ago, so there's just me and my son and daughter. I'm delighted to say I've got them into a very good school round here, though, and, most importantly for me, a daily help to stop the whole place becoming like a pigsty!'

They all laughed, appreciating the man's effort not to dwell on his tragedy but to be positive.

'We'll have to show you the sights of Sellingford, then,' said Iona with a smile. 'And I think I know most of the entertainment that's going on round here for children, having taken my nephews on a few outings!'

'I'll certainly hold you to that,' remarked Terry, shooting her an appreciative glance. 'And I know Luke and Verity would like someone other than just their old dad taking them on trips.'

After dinner there were the speeches, eminent men in the world of medicine getting up to say a few complimentary words about Professor Carter and then Matt's father himself rising to say very emphatically that he was not giving a speech—just a huge thank you to all the people who had helped and supported him throughout his career, especially his wife.

'Everyone,' he said fondly, looking down at his pretty wife, 'should be as lucky as I have been to have had the love of a good woman!'

There was a prolonged burst of applause, and then the band struck up again with a lively medley of modern tunes. The older contingent drifted away to other, quieter rooms, and Matt pulled Iona up from her chair.

'Come on, let's just have a final dance,' he murmured.

The evening was drawing to a close, but Iona felt as lively as she had at the start, excitement thrilling through her at being so close to Matt, his presence acting as potently on her as the champagne had.

She made her way to the cloakroom before they left, to pick up the cream pashmina she'd brought with her instead of a coat. There were quite a few women brushing their hair and renewing their lipstick. One of the older ones turned to Iona and smiled.

'You looked as though you were having a good time—you and Matt Carter made a very handsome couple on the dance floor!'

Another woman chimed in. 'Who wouldn't have a good time with Matt, he's every woman's dream, isn't he? I hope he's less of a flirt than his father was!'

The first woman looked rather embarrassed. 'Don't be silly, Daphne—I could see from his expression that Matt was mad about his partner!'

Iona laughed. She didn't mind what was said about Matt—she knew how happy she felt, and she was sure he felt pretty much the same way!

She had arranged to meet Matt outside the front door while he got the car. She stood in the balmy evening air, enjoying the banter and laughter of people leaving at the end of a wonderful evening. Matt had obviously not been able to collect his car immediately—she could see him talking to his father at the side of the house. Father and son seemed to be having a close discussion and, although she moved nearer, Iona didn't like to interrupt them. It was only gradually that what Professor Carter was saying to his son in his deep, carrying voice began to filter through to Iona's hearing—and only gradually that a cold feeling of disbelief began to freeze her heart.

'I must say, my boy, your mother and I are delighted that you seem to have taken our advice—the £500,000 I offered you to settle down before you went on that stupid jaunt to Mozambique seems to have concentrated your mind wonderfully! It's about time we had some grandchildren so I hope you damn well get on with it and set the date for the wedding! Remember, the day you have your first child will mean another half-million—so don't delay! It should be no hardship. She's a very beautiful girl—and bright with it—make a wonderful mother!'

Iona couldn't hear Matt's reply over the sudden sound of slamming car doors and people chattering. Matt's exchange seemed to be very short, for a second later he wheeled on his feet and marched off towards where he'd parked his car.

Iona stared after him, a numb feeling of revulsion creeping over her, and for a second the world seemed to spin around as if she was going to faint. It was as if she'd been struck with a bolt of lightning—the ghastly revelation that she'd obviously been living in cloud cuckoo land for the past week or so, certain that Matt had fallen for her as she had for him. What a fool she'd been! It was true he'd never actually said he loved her, but by his whole attitude and demeanour towards her there surely could have been no doubt about it?

The happy picture had begun to crack—the jigsaw had disintegrated before the final piece had been put in. Now she could see the true nature of this man, she thought bitterly. He didn't love her at all—he had chased her for the sole purpose of extracting money from his father. He'd implied several times that he was hard up—buying a new cottage and now a new car. How useful, then, to accept his father's inducement!

Cold fingers of bitterness curled round Iona's heart—how very convenient for Matt to receive money from his parents at this time! And how hopelessly naïve she'd been to believe that Matt could ever fall for anyone—he was a gigolo and always had been, and she'd fallen for his charm again, hook, line and sinker!

She stepped back into the shadows of the bougainvillea that twined round the archway of the huge portico round the front door and pulled her pashmina round her closely, suddenly shivering although the air was warm. Tears of anger mingled with self-pity welled up in her eyes. She wasn't the best at choosing men, it was obvious. Now she'd picked a man who had chosen her because he needed a breeding machine—someone suitable who would act as a source of income just when he needed it!

Matt's car drew up in front of the entrance and Iona stepped out of the shadows and got in beside him.

He turned to her before moving off again and put a gentle hand on her knee, looking at her with his warm grey eyes. 'Some evening, wasn't it?' he said in his deep voice. 'And my parents thought you were wonderful, too!'

'That's good.' Iona smoothed her dress with a trembling hand and looked straight ahead so that Matt couldn't see the bright tears in her eyes. 'I'm glad I came up to scratch!'

The car sped on through the dark night and Iona slid a look at Matt's strong profile so close to her.

How well he masked his cynical approach to love! She clenched her fists beside her and swallowed the annoying lump that had formed in her throat. Those few devastating words she'd heard Matt's father say had changed her future in the twinkling of an eye from exciting to bleak. A mixture of disbelief and shock whirled crazily in her mind, but one thing was certain—no way was she going to allow herself to be ground down by this. If Matt Carter thought he had made an easy conquest, he had another think coming!

CHAPTER EIGHT

'So, how was the Prof's leaving do—a night of wine and roses?'

Chloe looked up from the notes she was scrolling through on the computer to where Iona sat, apparently immersed in a medical journal.

Iona looked up, her voice studiously casual. 'What? Oh…yes, it was good. It was a really beautiful setting. The house is gorgeous, stuffed with antiques, with a wonderful sweeping staircase down to the hall and magnificent summer flowers everywhere…'

Chloe raised her eyebrows and said scornfully, 'Is that all you can say? I'm talking romance here, not a description of interiors for *House and Garden*. What about you and Matt—did this amazing setting produce the right ambience?'

Iona stood up and stretched. 'I don't know what you're getting at. I was Matt's partner for the night and we had a nice time—that's as far as it went, I assure you.'

She tossed the journal down on the desk and walked briskly out of the room. Chloe gazed after her with her mouth open, then she shook her head sadly and said to no one in particular, 'What's up with her? So she had a "nice time"? She makes the evening sound as exciting as a night out at a bowls club!'

Iona marched to Reception, her heart thudding, trying to compose herself. No way was she going to reveal to anybody just how wretched and furious she felt. What a gullible fool she was—knowing what Matt Carter was like, she'd still allowed herself to believe that he cared for her! The man had treated her like a commodity who could be traded for hard cash, and now she knew the full extent of his cynical approach to marriage she was no longer surprised he hadn't said he loved her. Obviously the inducement offered by his father to settle down was the prime reason he was taking her out—after all, she thought bitterly, she *was* eminently suitable!

Iona blinked back hot, angry tears and gritted her teeth. No way was she going to allow this setback to ruin her life—somehow she'd come through it like she had other disasters. She smiled cheerfully at Bet Lucas, who was busy writing up on the whiteboard which patients were in the different cubicles.

'Ah, just the person!' exclaimed Bet. 'There's a patient in cubicle three with acute abdominal pain—could you look at her, please, Dr Bellamy? Her husband's with her.'

Iona nodded and went in almost eagerly—the only thing that could take her mind off Matt was to plunge herself into work and stop thinking about her own heartbreak.

Susan Dainton's face was white and pinched, with beads of perspiration on her forehead, her mouth grimacing in pain. Her husband stood nervously by her side, clutching her hand in his and stroking her cheek. He looked intensely relieved when Iona came in.

'You'll be all right now, Sue—the doc's here!' he said, his expression lightening considerably. 'She'll know what's wrong.'

It was a curious thing that just the appearance of the doctor could make people feel better sometimes, thought Iona wryly, wishing that something as simple as that could help *her* wounded feelings. Determinedly she pushed all thoughts of Matt aside, and looked down kindly at the drawn face of her patient.

'Can you show me where this pain is, Mrs Dainton? Is it low down in your tummy, in the middle or to one side?'

'Low down, in the middle,' whispered the woman, barely audibly.

'It's been terrible,' interjected the husband, his voice rising with anxiety. 'All day she's been in agony. Can you give her something for it? Do you think it could be appendicitis?'

'We can do a variety of tests to try and find the cause,' reassured Iona. 'First of all, let me feel your abdomen, Mrs Dainton…'

'Be very gentle,' croaked the woman, looking at Iona in distress. 'I can't bear you to touch it…'

'I will be gentle and it won't take a minute,' promised Iona, pulling back the blanket that was over the woman.

She palpated the tense lower and upper abdomen with great care, and watched her patient's face as she did so for any reaction. Then she gently replaced the blanket and her mouth twitched in an amused smile.

'I think we can discount one theory—I'm pretty sure it's not your appendix,' she observed. 'There's a neat little scar there that shows you had it taken out some time ago!'

'Yes…of course,' gasped the woman. 'When I was quite young—I'd almost forgotten with all this pain.'

'Then is there a chance you could be pregnant?' Iona asked casually.

'Absolutely not,' answered her husband swiftly. 'I

had a vasectomy over a year ago now. Two kids are more than enough on our income!'

Iona's glance rested for a moment on Sue Dainton's face, and she frowned. Briefly she had seen a look of fear in the woman's eyes, and an almost pleading expression that said as plainly to Iona as if the woman had shouted it out, Please can I talk to you alone?

'I think we'll ask for an ultrasound scan—that could show up an ovarian cyst, or possibly other conditions that could give rise to this pain,' she said briskly, then she turned to Mr Dainton. 'I'll just go and arrange for a bed in Obs and Gynae so that they can book a scan as quickly as possible. When I return for your wife, perhaps you would like a cup of tea while you wait?'

'Can't I go with her for the scan?' asked the man.

'The consultant gynaecologist or the registrar will do the ultrasound and possibly a laparoscopy—that is, looking directly into the abdomen with a small viewing device. Of course, she'll be in Theatre for that, and while she's there I'm sure you could do with a break,' suggested Iona smoothly. 'You may have quite a lot to do later on!'

This time there was no mistaking the grateful look Sue Dainton flashed at her as she hurried out. There was no doubt that the patient wanted her husband out of the way whilst she spoke to Iona alone.

A few seconds later Iona returned. 'All fixed!' she said. 'You'll have a scan fairly soon—so if you would go and have some refreshment, Mr Dainton, I'll just ask your wife a few more questions.'

Iona's voice held an air of quiet authority, and Mr Dainton rose obediently.

'I'll go and ring my mother-in-law, then—she's looking after the children. See you later, pet!'

He gave his wife a peck on the cheek and went out, looking relieved that the responsibility of his wife could be handed over to someone else.

Iona turned to the young woman, who was watching her with anxious eyes, and said quietly, 'I notice that you've been bleeding—when did you last have a period?'

'Quite a few weeks ago,' Mrs Dainton whispered.

'So you may have suspected you could be pregnant?'

There was a long silence and the patient plucked at the blanket on top of her nervously. Iona patted her hand reassuringly.

'I don't want to pry—and it's completely up to you what information you wish to tell your husband. Anything you tell me is absolutely confidential—but if it helps us to diagnose your condition it would be very helpful,' Iona explained gently. 'You see, I'm concerned you could have what's called an ectopic pregnancy, and the bleeding may be coming from one of your Fallopian tubes. That could be a dangerous situation.'

'Why?' The woman's voice was tremulous.

'Sometimes a fertilised egg can lodge there instead of in the uterus—then as it expands and grows it can rupture the surrounding tissue, and that can lead to serious complications.'

Sue Dainton turned stricken eyes to Iona. 'I...I don't know what to say,' she stammered weakly. 'Andrew had a vasectomy—we agreed we didn't want any more children, but things haven't been too good between us recently. I...I've been seeing someone else.'

'So there is a chance you could be pregnant?'

The woman gave a huge sob and turned her face to the wall, tears streaming down her eyes. 'Oh. God, I suppose so, but I don't know how I can tell Andrew—he'll never forgive me!'

'We'll do a pregnancy test first, and together with the ultrasound we'll be able to ascertain if you really are pregnant. The consultant will probably do a laparoscopy to confirm the ectopic diagnosis.'

'And what will happen if it is?'

'You'll have an operation to remove the growing egg—which, I'm afraid, would not be viable anyway. The consultant will explain everything in detail.'

Sue Dainton gave a low moan as another spasm of acute pain gripped her. 'Will...will you tell my husband?' she muttered.

Iona held her hand gently. 'The consultant will speak to him when he has definite results—but only if you're absolutely sure that's what you want. It might be better, depending on the outcome, that your husband hears it from you.'

The woman looked miserably at Iona. 'I've been a fool, haven't I?'

Iona gave a grim smile. 'We all make fools of ourselves sometimes,' she murmured, then added briskly, 'The first thing is for you to get better and be relieved of this horrible pain. Try not to worry.'

The woman didn't reply, just hunched up under her blanket with her eyes closed. As she was wheeled down the corridor her husband came back to the cubicle clutching a polystyrene cup of coffee. He looked hopefully at Iona.

'Found out what it is yet?' he said brightly.

'Not yet. As I said, the gynaecologist is going to look at your wife and he'll have a word with you later. I should go and wait in the gynae ward visitors' lounge, then you'll be on hand when he's finished.'

Watching the man walk away, Iona felt a sudden sadness overcome her. In an hour or two the man's world would be shattered if, as she thought, his wife had been pregnant and she chose to tell her husband. And how many other lives would affected by Sue Dainton's infidelity? Iona paused for a second, her pen hovering over the notes she'd made on the woman, and her thoughts drifted to Matt. Sometimes, she reflected savagely, love makes fools of everyone.

She looked up as Jan's cheery little face peeped round the cubicle curtain.

'You're needed in cubicle one now,' she informed Iona. 'A teenage boy's been brought in—he's not looking too good. Heart's tachycardic and he's semi-conscious.'

Iona sighed. At least the flow of patients didn't allow her to dwell too much on her own dilemmas. She and Jan made their way to the first cubicle and Iona had to stop herself from taking a sharp intake of breath when she realised too late that Matt was also there, listening to the boy's chest. She compressed her lips. She would be politely professional, and that was all. No need for small talk, and positively no need to dwell on the fact that even from the back he looked heart-tuggingly attractive, his hair slightly rumpled and growing rather too long over the collar of his white coat. Briefly she closed her eyes, trying to block out the picture of her arms twined round Matt's neck only yesterday, completely confident and safe in the assumption that he loved her…

What a horrible irony it was that at the height of her happiness it had been dashed away by a half-heard conversation. It seemed incredible that someone as kindly and gentle as Matt could have treated her so cruelly, that she must never again let that muscular, demanding body press against hers or allow herself to taste his teasing persuasive lips.

Then Professor Carter's words echoed again in her head. 'The £500,000 I offered you to settle down… seems to have concentrated your mind wonderfully.' Her heart steeled. She felt completely devastated and empty. No matter how hard it was, their relationship was over—kaput! She took up a position near the bed and tried to control her trembling body.

Matt started palpating the patient's abdomen, and the boy stirred and mumbled incoherently. He looked round as Jan and Iona came near him, and said quietly to them, 'This young man's heart's palpitating and he's had difficulty breathing. His friend here, Maria, was with him and called an ambulance.'

In a corner was a phlegmatic-looking girl, her jaws moving stolidly on some chewing gum as she watched Matt dealing with her friend.

'Did you say you've been at an all-night party?' Matt said to her. 'Had a lot to drink?'

The girl shrugged. 'Had a few, I reckon. Bugsy likes his booze. We'd all come back to the flat and had something to eat about half an hour ago—and a short while after that he started gasping for breath.'

'Any other symptoms?' asked Iona.

'Well, the choking made his eyes stream. We thought he was a goner…'

Matt listened to Bugsy's chest again and raised his brows slightly. 'You have a listen, Dr Bellamy,' he said. 'His heartbeat seems almost normal now…strange!'

Iona listened carefully to the patient's heart and nodded. 'He seems to be calming down now. I wonder…what did you have to eat?'

'I had some chicken chow mein left over from the day before so we heated it up. Has he got food poisoning?'

Iona's eyes lit up as if she'd just thought of something, and she shook her head. 'I don't think it's food poisoning—probably more of a reaction, a kind of allergy. The reheated food could have caused a build-up in concentration of monosodium glutamate—that's a flavour enhancer. With a high level of alcohol this sort of extreme reaction can occur.'

Matt gave a little chuckle. 'I think you've hit the nail on the head!'

'I've never heard of that before!' said Jan. 'That's something else to worry about now—we're at risk even when we go and have a Chinese meal!'

Iona laughed. 'Only if you reheat it and have it on top of a load of alcohol!'

'Hell!' said Bugsy's companion slowly. 'So what happens now?'

'Plenty of water when he's come round should do the trick,' said Matt. 'We'll keep an eye on him here and let you know when he's feeling better if you sit in the reception area.'

Matt turned dancing eyes towards Iona. 'Well done, Dr Bellamy!' he said. 'You should have done forensic medicine!'

'Thanks. I have seen this condition once or twice

before when I was a student and people seemed to live off Chinese take-aways.' Iona's voice was off-hand, rather cool, and Matt looked at her sharply.

'You OK? Still recovering from last night?'

For a second Iona's glance wavered from his, then she looked back at him steadily. 'I suppose I am a bit...'

'Come round my place tonight, then. I'll cook you something delicious—guaranteed to make you feel better!'

It would take a lot more than that to make her feel better, thought Iona grimly. She took a deep breath and said tersely, 'I don't think so. I'm planning an early night...'

Matt looked slightly taken aback. 'Oh—right. Perhaps tomorrow?'

A thumping heart made it difficult for Iona to speak without sounding breathless. 'I'm not sure. I've got a pretty full schedule this week. I'd rather keep things free at the moment.'

She was almost pleased at the puzzled look that crossed his face. Then he frowned. 'I see,' he said slowly. 'If that's what you want...it has been a very busy week. I'll be in touch then very soon and we'll organise something together.'

His warm grey eyes searched hers for a second as if seeking an explanation, but Iona didn't answer, just watched him walk off slowly down the corridor.

'Think what you like, Matt Carter,' she muttered viciously to herself, 'but don't for a moment suppose we have anything going between us any more!'

She wheeled round and started to walk briskly towards the kitchen, suddenly longing for a restoring hot drink, and found herself crashing into a figure coming in the opposite direction.

'Whoa!' said a friendly male voice, catching her arms and holding her steady. 'You're obviously in a hurry!'

'What? Oh, sorry…' She squinted up at the man in front of her, recognising him from the night before. 'It's Terry, isn't it? Terry Cummings?'

He smiled down at her. 'Sure is—we met last night at that splendid dinner. I said I was coming to see your department soon—I didn't know it would be so forcibly!'

Iona looked at him wryly. 'I'm afraid I'm so desperate for a coffee I didn't look where I was going.'

'Then let's have one together,' said Terry. 'You sound as if you've had a pretty hard day so far!'

'Yes,' admitted Iona, with feeling, 'You could say that!'

There was some coffee simmering in the percolator and Terry poured out two mugfuls, handing one to Iona.

'You look rather tired,' he said, his gaze sweeping over her drawn face and heavy eyes. 'I guess late nights and work don't mix too well. But it was a marvellous occasion, wasn't it? Certainly one to remember!'

'Yes, it was quite an evening,' said Iona hollowly. 'I won't forget it in a hurry.'

'And such a wonderful setting!' continued Terry enthusiastically.

Iona smiled weakly and tried to look more interested, but stiffened when the door opened and Matt walked in. This, she thought despondently, was how it was going to be every working day from now on.

She'd never be able to escape from Matt's presence—
and that would make it very difficult to put him out
of her mind!

Matt nodded politely to Terry then turned to Iona
with a bright smile. 'Ah, here you are,' he remarked.
'I forgot to tell you I found this on the passenger seat
of the car after I'd dropped you off last night.'

He held out his hand and gave her a pearl drop
earring—one of a pair she'd been wearing. He smiled
engagingly at her. 'I'm sure you wouldn't have
wanted to lose it.'

'Thank you,' she said politely, taking it without
further comment.

'We were just saying how much we enjoyed your
father's retirement party,' said Terry genially. He
waved the coffee-pot at Matt. 'Want a cup? You seem
to have been very busy this morning. I think poor
Iona's dead on her feet—too much dancing, I think!'

Matt looked at Iona and for a second his twinkling
grey eyes locked with hers. She felt a flutter of agitation and looked hastily away.

'Well worth it, though, wasn't it? The band, and
everything else, was great,' he remarked, still watching her. Then he turned back to Terry courteously.
'And, yes, please, I'd like a coffee.'

As he put out his hand for the mug his bleeper went
off. 'Damn the wretched thing—I guess I'd better
have the coffee later.' He looked at Iona. 'Before I
go, I ought to have mentioned that my parents would
like to meet you again very soon. They wondered if
you'd be able to come for lunch next weekend—you
are off, aren't you?'

Iona bit her lip. How difficult this was! 'I don't

think I'll be able to,' she said carefully. 'I'll probably be away…er, seeing some old school friends.'

A look of disappointment flicked across Matt's face. 'Oh, that's a shame. Never mind, we can always fix something else up—but they're very keen to see you again. My father was rather bowled over, I think!'

Iona gave a stiff little smile and said vaguely, 'That would be nice.'

Matt paused at the door for a moment before he went out, looking back at Iona. If she hadn't known better, Iona thought miserably, she'd have sworn there was a look of genuine love and affection mixed with bewilderment in his warm eyes as if he had a sudden sense that all was not well between them. Her heart gave a jolt of sympathy, and she had an irrational longing to fling her arms round his neck and tell him that it was OK and that everything was fine and she loved him to bits. Then she gritted her teeth and picked up a magazine nonchalantly from the table and pretended to flick through it. When she looked up, Matt had gone.

If Terry had noticed an atmosphere between Iona and Matt he didn't give any sign of it, just said casually, 'So I take it that you and Matt Carter are an item? Been going together for some time?'

Iona gave a light laugh. 'What? Me and Matt? No, there's absolutely nothing between us. We're colleagues, that's all—worked in one or two places together.'

Terry's face brightened. 'Ah, so you, er, aren't involved with anyone at the moment?'

She shook her head. 'No—not now,' she said tersely.

'In that case, could I be very cheeky and ask you something?'

Iona dragged her thoughts from Matt. 'Of course, what is it?'

'I mentioned that my kids and I like cycling—any chance you could be our guide in the near future and show us the countryside around here?'

Iona looked at him speculatively. Poor man—it must be hard to be a single parent in a new place with young children. He was a pleasant man, pleasant but rather dull, and surely it could do no harm to help him out some time. After all, she had all the free time in the world now, hadn't she?

'Of course,' she said lightly. 'Next time I'm free.'

'I'll hold you to that,' Terry said with a smile. 'But I take it this weekend's no good from what you said to Matt Carter?'

'Er...no. I'm probably going to be away.'

Iona closed her eyes briefly, trying to shut out the thought of future weekends all horribly empty and lonely. However, she thought firmly, she really would go and see an old school friend—she needed to get away for a day or two and recharge her batteries. Organising something would help push the heartbreak over Matt to the back of her mind.

It was Sod's Law, Iona thought viciously as she tried to start her car for the umpteenth time, that, having set up a really good two days away in the country with one of her oldest friends, her car would let her down—it was as dead as a dodo! She got out of the driver's seat and looked at it crossly, giving the wheel a quick kick to relieve her feelings.

'How could you?' she muttered, feeling slightly

guilty over the fact that she should have taken it in for a service some time ago.

There was no way she could go to Christine's now as she was unlikely to get the car fixed at this late time, and public transport was something that didn't happen in Christine's remote part of the world. Iona tried to be positive. A change of plans didn't mean she would have to sit at home doing nothing—a brisk walk to the old castle on top of the hill would do her good and then she would mow the lawn and do some essential tidying up in the garden.

Iona rang Christine and explained her predicament, then set out for the castle, a medieval ruin situated high above Sellingford. It was a beautiful soft summer's day, with the sun just beginning to glow warmly on her back as she walked up the country lane that led to the hillside path. There was a low murmuring of bees working their way through the hedgerow flowers, and a faint smell of may blossom and elderflower drifted elusively in the air. Somewhere up in the blue sky a lark was singing its heart out, and Iona started to walk more briskly, feeling a sudden sense of purpose and renewed energy. What the hell did it matter if Matt Carter had fooled her into thinking he loved her? Life was still sweet—she had a job she loved and lots of friends. There were plenty of other fish in the sea, as Chloe was fond of saying, and she would get over this episode and forget soon enough how drop-dead gorgeous he was… wouldn't she?

She was passing the small row of terraced cottages that were just at the start of the climb up the hill. Two young children were cycling round and round the lane in front, trying various stunts, raising their front wheels off the ground, then doing a steep skid to a stop. Probably brother and sister, thought Iona, smiling as she watched their antics. They could even have been twins as they were practically the same size.

'Verity! Luke! Come and have some apple juice if you want,' called a voice from the porch of the cottage.

Iona looked across at the owner of the voice and saw to her surprise that it was Terry Cummings. He recognised her immediately and came over to her with a welcoming smile.

'Well—isn't this great? I didn't know you lived near here!' He looked across at his children, now staring at her with interest. 'Let me introduce you to Verity and Luke. Come here, children, and meet Dr. Iona Bellamy.'

The boy and girl were about eight years old, with round solemn faces and equally round metal-rimmed glasses at the end of turned-up noses. Verity had neat little pigtails sticking out on either side of her head and Luke had short hair that stood up in spikes. Iona's heart went out to them—and their father. It must be hard for all of them, having no mother or wife to guide and help them. Suddenly her problems seemed of less significance. After all, she was used to being on her own, and who knew what the future might bring?

'Hello,' she said, smiling at them. 'You look very good at doing tricks on those bikes of yours.'

They smiled back a little shyly and Terry said, 'How about a drink—coffee, or even apple juice?'

'An apple juice would be great.' Iona accepted gratefully. The unaccustomed walking had made her feel very thirsty and, anyway, she felt it would be churlish to refuse.

Terry soon came out with some glasses of juice on a tray and a few plain biscuits.

'Look,' he said eagerly. 'I've had a great idea. You know you said you'd come a bike ride with us some time—how about now? It's lovely weather, and when we've had enough we could go to a pub for some lunch.' He paused for a second, looking at her hopefully and then across at Verity and Luke. 'I know you kids would love that too, wouldn't you?'

Sudden animation crossed his children's faces and they beamed happily. 'Yes!' they shouted in unison. 'Let's go!'

'Well…why not? My plans to see my friend have fallen through anyway,' remarked Iona, then she chuckled. 'Not sure how I'll join you, though, unless I ride on the crossbar—I've not got a bike!'

Apparently that was no problem. They seemed to have one or two spare bikes in an old garden shed, and one was soon brought out, having been thoroughly inspected for safety by Terry.

In no time at all they were cycling off down the lane—Iona slightly hesitantly at first. They made their way towards the river, the children losing their shyness and shouting encouragement to the grown-ups, who followed more staidly and slowly behind. Iona watched their enthusiastic little figures racing ahead of her and reflected wryly that one couldn't stay gloomy for long where children were concerned.

Much to her surprise, it had turned out to be an enjoyable morning, reflected Iona. The four of them cycled for about an hour, a circular route that had taken them back to the pub where she and Matt had gone on their first real date. Iona tried to put that thought out of her mind. This was quite a different occasion, she told herself firmly, trying not to remember the lashing rain and the wet car, and how she and Matt had kissed each other so fervently, and later, done more than kiss...

'I suppose you know the Jolly Miller—it seems quite a popular place,' said Terry, interrupting her thoughts and propping his bike with the others against a wall.

He fiddled in his pockets for some money and turned to the children. 'Go in and get us some nice long drinks—and order us some food. Sandwiches all right?' he asked Iona.

She nodded. 'That would be great. Why don't we sit down here and wait for the kids to bring the food out?'

They sat under the shade of an umbrella over their table and watched life around the river go by—small barges, joggers running on the path, even the occasional rider plodding by on a horse. It was all very pleasant and relaxing.

Terry started to tell her of his career so far and how his children were settling down at their new school. Iona tried to concentrate on what he was saying and show interest, but her mind began to drift back to the evening she'd spent with Matt at this same pub, and how they'd first started to get to know each other. She tried to blank out the electric tension there'd been between them, and their closeness later that evening...then with a lurch she was brought back to reality as Terry's voice intruded into her thoughts.

'So you see,' he was explaining, 'I really feel a

small village school will be better for the children than the large one they were going to before…'

'Of course,' Iona agreed, guilty that she hadn't been giving him her full attention before.

She made an effort to talk animatedly to Terry and never noticed a lone figure in a corner of the pub's crowded garden watching her intently.

At first Matt couldn't believe it was Iona—after all, she was supposed to be away for the weekend. It just had to be someone very like her, with russet hair tied up in a ponytail and the same slender figure—strange how alike some people could be from a distance. He frowned as he took a draught of beer. He hadn't been able to put his finger on it, but over the last few days he'd felt a subtle change between Iona and himself, and the wonderful intimacy that they'd had seemed to have cooled over the last few days. That's why he'd come to have a quiet drink, to mull over what might have gone wrong. Had he said something to upset her—or perhaps he'd been taking things too fast? He sighed. When they were together it was hard to believe that there had been anyone else in their lives, but, of course, Iona was still recovering from an ill-judged relationship and probably she was being cautious. He would have to hold back and not rush things—telling her that his parents were looking forward to meeting her again had probably frightened her!

It had all been going so well. He couldn't believe how incredibly lucky he'd been to find someone so wonderful and beautiful after all the heartache he'd had in Africa. He'd thought he would never find any-one—hadn't really wanted to, because he liked being fancy-free and leading a bachelor existence. Then all at once Iona Bellamy had reappeared in his life and somehow he could think of no one else, imagine no future without her. And the wonderful thing was—he was sure that she had felt the same about him. There was no mistaking the magnetic attraction they had for each other—making love had been so wonderful. He smiled to himself, remembering how they had decided to take a few days off in the next few weeks and spend most of it in bed!

He watched as the woman with a strong resemblance to Iona turned round to look up at the children coming back with some food, and suddenly he realised with a shock that it *was* actually her after all!

Matt gazed in astonishment at Iona. What the hell was she doing here with that Terry Cummings when she'd told Matt she couldn't see him? He stood up in order to see her better—no mistake, that glowing hair and the wide hazel eyes could only belong to Iona.

'I just don't get it,' he muttered. 'I thought this was the weekend she was seeing her old mates. It seems she rather misled me there!'

Then his face softened. Iona wouldn't deliberately deceive him—she wasn't devious by nature. Perhaps she and Cummings had bumped into each other by accident. He pushed his way through the tables with couples and families sitting round them and went towards her. Terry Cummings was leaning forward and smiling at her.

'It's been the most marvellous morning,' he was saying. 'I'm so glad you managed to come. I look forward to the next time!'

Matt's jaw tightened, and a cold feeling of bitterness went through him. What the hell was happening?

The whole thing sounded prearranged! He stopped and stared at the little tableau with incredulity and fury, suddenly convinced that he had been betrayed. No wonder Iona's manner towards him had been strained in the past few days. She'd obviously had her eye on Terry Cummings—and it hadn't taken her long to latch onto him, he reflected savagely.

In angry bewilderment he watched Iona and Terry laugh and talk to the two children, then with a scowl he turned abruptly on his heel and strode off towards Sellingford.

She's not going to cast me off that lightly, he thought furiously. Come Monday morning, however hectic, Dr. Iona Bellamy is going to have some explaining to do!

CHAPTER NINE

IONA was beginning to wish she'd never agreed to go cycling with the Cummings family. Fun though it had been, Terry had twice been on the phone the next day to see if she would go with them on some other outing. She had a horrible feeling that he was rather too keen to get to know her on more than just a casual basis, and she had no wish to encourage anything like that. She was through with relationships for a long time, she thought grimly as she walked into Reception.

The room was crowded with the usual mixture of humanity. Out of the corner of her eye Iona could see Matt talking to one of the consultants. Quickly she turned away from him and to Connie, the receptionist. Connie was using all her diplomatic skills to deal with a demanding parent holding a crying child and a plump man insisting he be seen immediately as he had a plane to catch.

The man swung round and accosted Iona as she came up to the desk.

'You a doctor?' he demanded aggressively. 'I've been waiting over an hour to have this ankle seen to—just how long will it be before I can be X-rayed? I've got a very important meeting to get to in London...'

Iona's mood was not conciliatory at the moment—she was too aware of Matt's presence, hearing that deep sexy voice in discussion just behind her. Inside, she felt a horrible empty sadness where a few days ago she would have been filled with the excitement of knowing someone she loved was so close. With something like despair she wondered how she could remain totally professional, working with him. No wonder she felt jumpy and irritable and that there was a certain terseness in her voice when she spoke to the man.

'Your name, please?'

'Wilkins—Ben Wilkins. It's imperative that—'

'You've been seen by the triage nurse, haven't you?'

'A brief look, yes. She said she didn't think it was broken, but that I'd need an X-ray. I must know how long all this will take.' His voice sounded slightly desperate. 'Perhaps I'd be better trying to get the plane and going to a hospital after the meeting if I can't be seen now.'

Iona bit back a remark to the effect that there were many more urgent cases to be seen first, and couldn't he see everyone was working flat out? Then something made her look more perceptively at the man's face, which was pale, a pulse beating hard in his neck. She noticed the trembling of his hand, the slight beads of perspiration on his forehead. He was clearly under a great deal of stress—and it could be that his ankle wasn't his only physical problem. Perhaps a lot hinged on this meeting—even his livelihood. It was her job to try and calm his agitation and, from the look of him, lower his blood pressure!

She gave a sudden sweet smile of reassurance. 'Look, Mr Wilkins, don't worry—I'll go and see now how long it will be until your slot. I know they're working flat out at the moment, but I can take you through to a cubicle where you can put your ankle up, and while you're waiting I'll have a look at it. I really think we ought to assess it before you go on a plane.'

Her soft touch seemed to mollify the man, and he looked a little abashed. 'I…I didn't mean to imply that I was the most important case here,' he said. 'It's just…well, such a lot hangs on this meeting and it will reflect really badly on me if I'm not there. I was beginning to think the staff here had forgotten all about me…'

He sat down heavily on a chair, mopping his brow, and Iona phoned through to X-ray, reporting back to the man that he would be seen in the next ten minutes and that a porter would bring through a wheelchair to take him to the cubicle.

Matt came up to Iona as she was following her patient. He had an unusual expression of irritation on his face.

'We've got an RTA expected in three minutes,' he said brusquely. 'I've already told Mr Wilkins he'll be seen in due course. We may need everyone we've got soon so, please, don't prioritise him.'

'I think Mr Wilkins may have more wrong with him than a sprained ankle,' Iona replied levelly, refusing to be bounced into abandoning the man. 'He seems very agitated…'

'They all do,' snapped Matt. 'Everyone wants to be seen first! The man's been triaged—he should bloody well wait his turn.'

Iona looked at him curiously. He didn't sound his usual unflappable self, open to reason and deflating dramas with a humorous word. After all, Casualty was often like this.

'Normally I would agree with you,' she said

smoothly, 'but I am concerned about Mr Wilkins's general condition. I feel very strongly that he should be checked out.' She paused for a second. 'You seem to be a little on edge,' she observed coldly.

A strange look came into Matt's eyes as he looked down at her, his glance raking her face. 'Maybe I am,' he said shortly. 'By the way, I'd like a word later before you go to lunch if you don't mind.'

Iona hesitated. This seemed less and less like the Matt she knew. There was a harsh, bitter tone about his voice, and she wondered if he suspected that things between them were not the same—in which case, perhaps it was as well to clear the air and tell him just why their little liaison was over.

'OK by me,' she said as casually as she could, with a constricting lump in her throat. 'And now I am going to see Mr Wilkins if you don't mind. There's something bugging me about that man's symptoms.'

There was a slight flush on her cheeks and an over-brightness of her hazel eyes which wasn't connected with her concerns for her patient. Matt was too perceptive not to notice. He gave a heavy sigh and touched her arm lightly.

'Sorry, Iona, I was a bit heavy with you there. But you're quite right—if you've any worries, the man should be monitored.' He made to move away, then paused and looked back at her, his voice softer. 'Don't forget, though, I need to see you just before lunch in the office.'

Iona felt the impression of his light touch as keenly as if he'd put an electric current through her arm. Only he could set her senses tingling like that, she thought sadly, and she couldn't imagine anyone else ever having that effect.

Just before she went into the cubicle to attend to Mr Wilkins she looked back at Matt, talking to Bet Lucas in the corridor, his tall figure distinctive against every other man in the building. Just how was she going to tell him it was all over, she quailed, when she knew she still loved and wanted him with every fibre of her being? Then an insistent inner voice said firmly, Remember you're just a commodity to him, Iona Bellamy—love doesn't enter into it with Matt Carter!

With renewed strength she swished open the curtains to examine her patient.

Ben Wilkins sat bolt upright on the bed, his anxious eyes first looking at his watch then flicking feverishly through text messages on his mobile.

'I'm afraid you can't use your mobile in the hospital,' warned Iona. 'Anyway, I just want to carry out a few checks on you.'

'Oh, dear,' he said fretfully. 'I've just learned my sales manager can't be at the meeting—it's even more important now that I get there.'

He grimaced and shifted uneasily on the bed, holding his left arm.

'What's the matter?' asked Iona as she wound a cuff round his upper right arm to take his blood pressure.

'Got a funny heavy feeling in the top of my chest, and my arm hurts,' he muttered, then he smiled wryly. 'I've had it before, actually—it always goes off after a while. It just seems sharper than usual.'

'Have you been to the doctor about it?' asked Iona, watching the mercury rise and fall in the sphygmomanometer.

'Haven't had time,' he admitted. 'My wife keeps

going on about me going, but with three kids to keep I can't afford to take time off work.'

Iona took out her stethoscope and hooked it into her ears, pressing it to his chest and listening intently for a minute. 'Your blood pressure's quite high—do you smoke?'

'Afraid I do—but not all that much,' he said defensively. Then he lifted his head and frowned. 'What's all this to do with my ankle?' he asked. 'Any joy on the X-ray being done soon?'

Iona stuffed her stethoscope back in her pocket. 'You're not going to like this,' she said gently, 'but I'd really like to do some more tests on you.'

'What kind of tests?'

'Mr. Wilkins, I suspect that you are having, or have had, an angina attack.'

The man looked at her, round-eyed. 'Angina? That's something to do with the heart, isn't it? Nothing to do with ankles.'

Iona smiled faintly. 'No, not ankles…it's pain in your chest when there's insufficient oxygen being carried to the heart via the blood. It can happen during exercise, or when you're stressed. You mentioned a few minutes ago that you felt a kind of heaviness in that area, and you've felt it before. Your blood pressure's rather high, and you've other symptoms which make me feel that we should run some blood tests, and that in the near future you should do a cardiac stress test.'

Expressions of alarm and incredulity flickered over Ben Wilkins's face, and he struggled to sit up.

'Have they time to do the tests before I get my plane? I've just got to get there,' he said desperately.

'I strongly advise you to stay. Look, what's more

important—your health or a meeting that surely someone else could take? Haven't you a deputy?'

He was silent for a minute, then he sighed and pulled out a piece of paper from a pocket. 'I suppose so. I'm always being told I should delegate more.' He looked anxiously at Iona. 'I'd have to ring this chap, but if I can't use my mobile…'

'I can bring a telephone in here for you and perhaps you could ring your wife, and she could get in touch with people for you.'

Ben's plump face looked gloomily at Iona. 'She doesn't even know I've twisted my ankle, let alone got a heart condition!' Then he lay back against the pillows for a minute with his eyes closed and gave a resigned sigh.

'You know,' he confided, 'I'm actually rather relieved it's come to this—I've been feeling under the weather for some time. Perhaps the twisted ankle's done me a favour!'

It was nearly lunchtime and, amazingly, there was a respite in the constant flow of patients. The RTA had been dealt with, two of the victims being sent to Theatre with serious leg wounds and another to a neurological unit at a nearby hospital. Iona started to enter some data into one of the computers situated in the bay opposite the cubicles and tried to ignore a headache which she was sure was due to tension—the meeting with Matt hung over her head like the sword of Damocles. For some reason she felt like a naughty schoolgirl about to see the headmaster—and what, she thought indignantly, had she done wrong? She could think of nothing disastrous at work, and when it came to their own relationship, surely Matt had deceived her completely?

She stiffened as she felt a hand on her shoulder and whipped round to see Matt's stony face looking down at her.

'Could I see you now?' he said. 'It seems a good time while we're quiet.'

Her heart fluttered, somehow sure that what he had to say would concern her attitude to him and afraid that she couldn't deal with it.

'I can't come yet,' she said. 'I've just got these notes to enter…'

He put a hand over hers, preventing her from using the keyboard. 'This won't take long,' he said firmly. 'It's important.'

He opened the office door and she went in.

He stood in front of her, his good-looking features hard and dark. 'What's going on?' he said.

A question she might well ask of him, thought Iona wryly. 'I don't know,' she parried. 'Perhaps you'd tell me.'

He folded his arms and looked down at her, a scathing expression in his eyes. 'You know darn well what I'm talking about—you and me—us! Things have changed—and rather suddenly. I'd like to know why.'

You arrogant git, thought Iona, trying to ignore the feelings that his powerful frame ignited in her when he was so close. He's blaming me for the disruption in our relationship. Wouldn't dream that it was something to do with him!

'I'd have thought it was quite obvious, Matt.'

'Not to me,' he said harshly. 'The last few weeks have been magical as far as I'm concerned,' he continued slowly. 'I thought they were for you, too. You can't deny that we had something special going. I thought...I thought we had a future together.'

Of course you did—you were counting on it weren't you? Iona's thoughts whizzed round in her head like ingredients in a mixer. Had he no *idea* how calculating he'd been?

He came towards her and put both arms on her shoulders. He was very close to her, so close she could smell the faint tang of aftershave, feel his warm breath on her cheek. He only needed to pull her fractionally nearer and they would be touching hip to hip, chest to chest. Her heart began to clatter alarmingly against her ribcage and she took a nervous step back, away from that tantalising body.

'Perhaps you assumed too much,' said Iona coldly.

There was an unfathomable expression in his eyes. 'Evidently,' he said shortly. 'I should have remembered that you cast off men as easily as you do your clothes.'

'What?' gasped Iona, hardly able to believe her own ears. Then outrage spilt into every vein, and her blood boiled with anger. 'I don't believe this! Of all the bloody effrontery! Are you implying that I just jump into bed with everybody?'

'Well, don't you? You certainly can't sustain relationships—look at the poor sod you let down on your wedding day. Just chucked him aside like an old glove, didn't you?'

'Don't you dare imply that I did that lightly,' said Iona through gritted teeth.

'And it didn't take you long to find someone else after you'd decided you'd tired of me,' Matt went on relentlessly, his eyes boring into her.

'That's simply ridiculous,' she snapped. 'But don't believe that you're the only fish in the sea—there must be plenty of men around who don't feel they're God's gift to women and have a certain humility in their relationships. Not that I have any intention of going out with anyone else—you've put me off that for a long time!'

He laughed mirthlessly. 'You seem to have taken quite a shine to Terry Cummings—perhaps you feel sorry for a poor widower in a strange place!'

Iona scowled at him in fury. 'I shan't even dignify that with an answer, Matt Carter. Although,' she added, 'if I want to be friendly with someone I don't think I need to ask your permission. Perhaps you'd better look to yourself to find out where our relationship hit the skids!'

His expression looked genuinely puzzled and he shook his head helplessly. 'It beats me,' he said simply. 'I thought we were the perfect couple—ideally matched. Then everything seemed to change overnight... What went wrong, Iona?'

Matt's voice had softened and his grey eyes looked into hers reproachfully. Iona turned her head away, although she felt a terrible urge to press her lips to his—but she wasn't going to be soft-soaped into falling for all that charm again. He was so terribly convincing—but, then, of course, that was a conman's stock in trade, wasn't it? He could obviously see £500,000 slipping from his grasp and was trying every trick in the book to retrieve it—from anger to gentle persuasion!

She tilted her chin and looked up at him defiantly, her russet hair catching the light as she shook it back. 'You know darn well that it takes two to have a loving relationship. You aren't motivated by anything as simple and unrewarding as love—you never have been! Oh, no, your motives are much more devious and materialistic than that, and I'm afraid I won't be a party to it!'

'What the hell do you mean—I don't love you?' He took a step towards her, imprisoning her against the wall, one arm on either side of her, making it impossible for her to go. 'I've no idea what the other garbage was that you're talking about—but perhaps this will convince you that I love you, want you, desire you more than any woman I've ever met.'

Before she could draw breath, his mouth was on hers in a demanding, bruising kiss, his hands were round the back of her head so that she couldn't move and his hard body was pressed to hers. She tried to struggle against him, her arms flailing against his back, trying to force him away from her.

It was too difficult, too difficult when his lips were fluttering down her neck and his hands were caressing her breasts with the lightest and most exquisite of touches. She couldn't help it, her arms went round his neck of their own volition, her insides melted into liquid desire and she knew that soon she would relinquish any pretence of not wanting him.

'Don't do this, Matt,' she whispered. 'You're doing it for the wrong reasons—just trying to seduce me into believing you love me. I don't want this...'

He looked down at her, his eyes wide with disbelief and humour. 'You seem to like it,' he observed, his voice husky. 'You've only to say the word, and we can be together always. We were meant for each other—even my father could see that!'

His father! The word galvanised Iona to super-

human effort, and with a grunt of fury she pushed
Matt away from her, wriggling out of his arms and
standing panting by the desk, her hazel eyes sparking
with anger.

'What's the matter now?' asked Matt in astonishment.

'I honestly don't care a toss what your father thinks
about me,' she spat out venomously. 'Obviously you
set great store by his opinion—after all, Daddy holds
the purse-strings, doesn't he?'

He came towards her again, his hands open as if
in disbelief. Iona took her hand back and slapped his
cheek as hard as she could.

'I'm not for sale, Matt Carter,' she said viciously.

She pushed passed him, leaving him rubbing his
face and looking after her in astonishment. As she
went to the door it opened and Chloe stepped in.

Iona almost ran out and Chloe looked after her
disappearing figure and back to Matt. A sardonic
smile crossed her face. 'Well, well,' she murmured,
'A lovers' tiff, or what?'

CHAPTER TEN

MATT CARTER was finding it hard to concentrate on the lecture that was in progress entitled 'The Effect of Drugs in the Community'. He knew all about their effects, he thought gloomily. He saw the consequences every day in the hospital—people having been mugged, rival gangs beating each other up, users in the grip of heroin. The list was endless. He didn't feel he needed a lecture to tell him what was going on—and, anyway, he was in no mood to sit still for an hour in the lecture hall, when two rows away from him sat Iona, her lovely profile looking studiously towards the platform and the speaker.

She knows I'm here, thought Matt, looking across at her in some despair. She's just ignoring me. He gripped the rail in front of him viciously so that his knuckles were white. Whatever Iona felt about him—and she'd made it pretty clear it wasn't very complimentary, he reflected ruefully—she'd got the wrong end of the stick. She seemed to think he was under his father's thumb completely. And just because his father liked her, she considered it an insult—as if he, Matt, didn't know his own mind!

But why had things changed so quickly between them? He shook his head in bewilderment, unable to believe that she really was the sort of woman who would flit from man to man. Surely Iona had left her fiancé because she hadn't been able to live a lie—just as he had broken up with Shelley in Africa. They had both tried to be honest, but his honesty had led to a tragedy, and he had come back home believing that he never wanted to or would be able to, commit himself to anyone. Far from his father influencing him in any way, he had always wanted to do his own thing, get away from that strong personality that had dominated most of his young life. Now, quite unexpectedly and wonderfully, he'd met the love of his life and he didn't give a damn whether his father liked her or not. What he did care about was holding onto Iona, whatever it took.

'I just don't understand how could she do this to me,' he muttered to himself, causing the man next to him to gaze at him curiously.

'Something the matter?' asked the man.

'No,' said Matt hollowly. 'Nothing at all.'

He could see Chloe sitting beside Iona and he gave a wry smile. Chloe's untimely entrance after Iona had left the office in such dramatic fashion had been slightly embarrassing but, being Chloe, she hadn't let the situation faze her.

'So what was that all about?' she'd demanded, fixing Matt with a stern eye. 'Did you take some liberties with madam?'

Matt, still stroking his cheek from the smart contact of Iona's hand, had shrugged helplessly. Unable to stop himself, he'd confessed wearily, 'I just don't know Chloe. I thought…I was sure that Iona and I had clicked. Dammit—we've had the most wonderful time. We were perfect for each other!'

Chloe had swivelled round in the chair she'd sat in and had looked at him thoughtfully. 'I don't know what's upset her either—but let me tell you this. I know Iona's mad about you. I've never seen her so besotted with anyone—her whole face lights up when you're around.'

'She didn't give me that impression just now,' Matt had said ruefully. 'She seems to think I'm taking her out for the wrong reasons. What can I do to convince her I love her to bits?'

'Don't give up on her, Matt,' Chloe had answered firmly. 'Whatever it is, Iona's got it all wrong. You've got to find out what's going on—and fast. You and she were meant to be together.'

And Chloe was right, Matt thought grimly. He wasn't going to give up. Even if there was a valid reason for Iona to hate him now he had to know what it was—before she was snapped up by someone else.

There was a scraping of feet and general shuffling as people got up from their seats. The lecture was over and it was time to start the night shift on Casualty. As Matt rose, Iona turned towards him on her way out and their eyes met for a second. There was a glint of steel in her look as if to say 'Keep away from me, Matt Carter—I meant what I said!'

He followed her down the corridor, determined that he wasn't going to let things drift any more. He would confront her again some time during the shift and he would somehow convince her that his father's opinion had nothing to do with how he felt about her. The longer she kept him at arm's length, the harder it would be to get together again.

Matt cursed softly as he saw Terry Cummings come out of the office and start talking animatedly to Iona. Why couldn't the wretched man leave her alone? He seemed to be all over her like a rash. Not that he could blame him, he thought savagely. Even in her hospital greens Iona looked delectable. He

watched her vivacious response to the hospital manager with resentment. She'd said she didn't want to
form another relationship again for a long time but,
looking at her, Matt wasn't so sure. Perhaps she saw
Cummings as a nice safe prospect—someone to go
out with without getting too involved. He started to
walk towards her when Terry moved away, but almost immediately a woman's hysterical voice could
be heard wailing piteously from the waiting area in
Reception.

'Help—please, help. Oh, my God, it's my sister…
Someone come and help me…'

The sound was frightened and desperate and Matt
pushed thoughts of Iona out of his head and sprinted
towards Reception, closely followed by other staff.
Even Colin the porter, usually the most sluggish of
men, was galvanised into life and trotted urgently
alongside Matt.

'What is it—what's happening?' demanded Matt of
the young white-faced woman standing shaking by
the automatic doors of Reception and sobbing for
help.

The girl pointed outside. 'L-L-Lucy's collapsed.
She can't seem to breathe, and I can't carry her myself. Please, please, hurry…'

Matt pushed past her and saw in the evening light
a huddled figure lying on the grass roundabout at the
entrance to Casualty and one or two anxious-looking
people bending over her. Matt didn't stop to ask any
other questions. He and Colin dashed over to the
stricken girl and both of them carried her swiftly back
up the small drive.

'We'll take her straight to the treatment room,'
gasped Matt. He'd had a cursory look at the victim's

face, and he didn't like what he saw. He could hear her laboured, choking breathing, see her lips, blue and swollen.

The two men lowered the patient onto the bed in the treatment room and Matt bent over her, quickly assessing her condition. The girl's sister hovered anxiously behind, making little noises of distress.

'Is she all right? Can you make her better? Why is she making that funny sound? What are you doing to her now?'

Iona had run into the room, automatically falling in as one of the team. She had raised the girl's feet and started to monitor her blood pressure. Her strong, calm tones cut through the girl's frightened edge-of-hysteria voice.

'I'm raising her legs to improve the blood flow to her lungs and heart—quite a usual procedure,' she assured her. 'Now, tell us—how long has she been like this? Did it start after something she'd done or eaten?'

'We...we'd just had an ice cream from the van opposite the hospital—only about five, ten minutes ago. We'd been visiting our nan in the hospital...'

'What kind of ice cream?' asked Matt tersely. 'What flavour?'

'Vanilla, with little bits of chocolate and nuts on the top,' whispered the girl.

'Do you know if she's ever had an allergy to nuts before?' asked Iona.

'No...I don't think so. Oh, God, she looks so terrible...'

Bet Lucas put a firm arm round the terrified girl's shoulders and said soothingly, 'You come with me, dear. Let the doctors get on with things. She's in good hands but they mustn't be distracted. What a good job you were so near help when this happened.'

She led her gently away from the scene where Lucy, her sister, lay perilously ill.

Matt looked up at Iona, his stethoscope dangling from his neck. 'Pupils dilated, tongue and throat swollen. Almost certainly anaphylactic shock. She needs adrenalin pronto.'

Iona nodded. 'Injecting it now…'

'Give her some Benadryl as well. I'll get this airway into her throat—don't want it closing up on us. Can you set up a saline drip? Don't give it until these drugs have taken effect.'

In a few seconds Jan had wheeled the saline drip over, and there was a tense silence in the room, everyone's eyes watching the girl's shaking body and blotchy swollen limbs, willing the drugs to reverse her symptoms. Matt assisted Lucy's breathing by pressing rhythmically on her chest and gradually the shaking of the patient's body began to subside, her breathing became less stertorous and started to achieve a rhythm of its own without Matt's help.

There was an almost collective sigh of relief round the room, and the tension lessened as Iona listened to Lucy's heart and checked her pulse.

'I think she's going to be OK,' she said quietly after a few minutes. 'We've been lucky.'

'Could you ring the medical ward, Jan, and get a bed? She'll have to be monitored for a day or two,' said Matt. 'Perhaps you could also go and get her sister—give her the good news!'

Matt and Iona were left alone monitoring the patient, who in a remarkably short space of time began to recover, the drugs reversing the allergic effect that the innocent consumption of an ice cream had had on her.

'Good result, wasn't it?' muttered Matt, his grey eyes watching Iona as she started up the saline drip which would prevent harmful reactions to the powerful drugs they had given the girl.

'Very,' replied Iona tersely, looking at him stonily. Then she turned away and smiled down at the young patient, whose eyes were now wide open. Iona held the girl's hand and said gently, 'I bet you feel a whole lot better now. I think you'd better keep off anything with nuts in it in future!'

The plastic airway down the girl's throat prevented her from saying anything, but she attempted to smile and squeezed Iona's hand. Then Colin came to take her to the medical ward where a careful watch would be kept on her for the next two days.

'Another satisfied customer,' remarked Matt, tucking his stethoscope in his top pocket and going towards the door. He turned back towards Iona and said rather enigmatically, 'Just goes to show that things you like can sometimes have a bad effect on you…'

Iona looked at him sharply. 'What do you mean by that?'

Matt smiled wryly at her. 'You should know. Didn't I have a bad reaction the other day from something I'm rather fond of?'

Iona reddened. 'You're referring to me, aren't you? What I did to you…' She looked down at her hands and bit her lip, then said in a rush, 'I'm sorry—I didn't mean to go over the top. I shouldn't have hit out at you.'

'You obviously felt very strongly that I'd behaved badly.'

She tilted her chin and looked at him challengingly. 'Well, so you did. I want someone to love me for myself—not for any other reason. Not because you've been bribed to have me.'

Matt looked at her in astonishment. 'Bribed? What the hell are you talking about?'

'Come off it, Matt. I know how attractive your father's inducement was. I'm worth quite a lot of money, aren't I? Half a million pounds isn't bad and another instalment when I produce the first child!'

The silence was deafening, and Matt's face hardened. 'What in heaven's name made you think that?' he demanded at last. Then a gleam of sudden intelligence shone in his eyes. 'You heard my father say that after his party didn't you?' He laughed shortly. 'And you believed it? Believed that I'd treat you as a sort of commodity to be bargained over?'

There was the sound of voices and footsteps outside the door. Iona flicked her hair back and shrugged. 'I'm not prepared to stay here and discuss this with the rest of the unit, but you finally seem to have cottoned onto just why you're no longer flavour of the month. You see, Matt, my price comes a little higher than half a million—I want to be loved for myself alone, not as a convenient bank roll because you've got into debt.'

His face as hard as granite, Matt strode forward and held her arm tightly. 'Iona, how could you be so silly? I've never heard anything so ridiculous in my life.'

Iona snatched her arm from his and stared at him defiantly. 'Let me go, Matt,' she said coldly. 'I don't think we have anything to say to each other any more. You and I are history.'

Then she twisted away from him, opened the door

without another word and marched out of the room and down the corridor. Matt gazed after her for a second, his eyes blazing, then he pushed past the surprised Bet and Jan and ran after her as she disappeared through the doors of Casualty and into the car park.

Iona almost sprinted down the drive and into the little wooded copse to the side of the hospital—anything to get away from Matt, so that she couldn't see him or hear him any more. Tears ran down her cheeks and she felt cold—cold with despair and unhappiness. She leant against a tree in the evening sunshine and tried to calm her shaking body, completely unaware of the soft, balmy air and the sweet smell of new-mown grass wafting up from the lawn by the hospital drive.

She hated rows! She couldn't believe that in the space of a few days she'd had the most terrible confrontations with the man she still loved with all her heart. It was true, she thought miserably, she couldn't switch off her feelings like one could a light bulb, and the fact was that, whatever he'd done, she couldn't stop loving Matt. She turned towards the tree and put her head in her arms, sobbing her heart out.

'It's over,' she whispered again and again to herself. 'It was so wonderful…and now I'll never feel his arms around me again…'

She pressed her forehead against the rough bark of the tree, trying to dull the agony in her mind, forcing herself to come to terms with the fact that she and Matt were finished.

Then she felt a gentle hand on her shoulder and a familiar voice said softly, 'Come on, my darling, don't let's finish on a sad note like this. We've got to talk, you and I.'

Iona looked slowly round, her heartbeat starting to gallop. Matt's face was gazing down at her with an expression of sadness mixed with tenderness. She shook her head wordlessly, unable to speak for the tears falling down her face. Matt put his arms round her and cradled her as he would have comforted a child, and she felt too emotionally drained to pull away, to tell him and his sweet-talking tongue to take a running jump.

Matt put his finger under her chin and held up her face to his. 'Did you really think I could be so calculating as to take my father up on his ridiculous offer? Didn't you hear what I replied to him?'

'No,' she gulped. 'There was too much noise.'

'Then you don't know all the facts, do you? It might interest you to know that I told him not to be so ridiculous, and to stop bribing me to do as he wished—I was a big boy now and would marry who I wanted.' Matt pulled Iona hard towards him. 'I also told him that I loved you and wanted to make my life with you, whether he flung money at me or not.'

Iona's eyes raked his face, trying to assess whether he was telling the truth, then she shook her head helplessly, that familiar feeling of arousal at his closeness distracting her.

'But…but you never told me before that you loved me,' she cried in despair, feeling the assured touch of his hand round the back of her neck, his other hand round her waist. 'You never actually *said* it. And when I heard your father and remembered how you were trying to buy your own place and the new car and everything, I thought how tempting his offer must seem.'

'Just goes to show you shouldn't jump to conclusions…I'm not completely penniless, you know.' Matt's strong hands had pulled her so close to him that she could feel the reverberation of his voice against her body. 'I should have realised that my father speaks very loudly and that you might have heard his daft suggestions. And the reason I never said I loved you, my darling, was because I didn't want to make another mistake.'

Iona's look was scornful, disbelieving. 'What do you mean—*another* mistake? Wasn't I just one more fool in a long line of easy conquests?'

Matt sighed and gave a shamefaced grin. 'I know I've got a reputation…I'm not proud of it. At one time it was fun to have a different girl on arm every day…'

'Or in your bed,' said Iona cynically. 'So what was this *other* mistake you made?'

'I had to be certain about your feelings for me. We'd both made a hash of relationships, it seems—mine led to tragedy.'

Iona looked at him in surprise. 'You'd led someone on like I had done with Kevin, you mean?'

Matt smiled faintly. 'I went out to Africa because the job sounded interesting, and I wanted to get away from my dear father's rather dominating influence for a while.'

And the bevy of women who'd fallen for you, thought Iona wryly.

'It was meant to be a light interlude in my life—I had no intention of settling down.'

'But you met someone there?' she prompted.

'Shelley was a nurse who'd also come from England and we hit it off straight away. She wanted to take things further than I did—in fact, she was determined we should get married. In a small community like that, emotions become rather intense...'

'You couldn't get away from her like you could in Sellingford?'

Matt nodded. 'That's right. I should have made it clear from the outset that ours was going to be a fun relationship while we were abroad, nothing permanent. When I did tell her, it was disastrous—I went about it completely the wrong way.'

His voice had fallen to a whisper, and a bleak look crept into his face as he stared over Iona's head to the hills beyond Sellingford. For a second they were silent, a lone blackbird singing his plaintive evening song in the tree above them.

'But what went wrong?' prompted Iona in a gentler voice. 'Why did it have such terrible consequences?'

'Because,' said Matt grimly, 'I informed her that there was no hope of us getting married, and we had a terrible row. I...I told her it might be better if we didn't see each other again and she rushed out onto the dirt track outside the building we were in. The car that was coming along didn't have a chance to avoid her. Her death was almost instantaneous. I should never have finished things so abruptly. I caused her death almost as much as if I'd been driving the car that hit her, and that's why I felt I couldn't stay there any more.'

Iona drew back and looked at the agony on his face, then she put up her hand hesitantly and stroked his cheek gently. 'It's not true that you caused her death,' she whispered, 'No one could have foreseen that. It was a tragedy that a car was coming just as she ran out, but in no way was it your fault.'

He looked down at her sadly. 'That's why I had to be very sure of both our feelings. I didn't want to hurt anyone else, even emotionally, and I knew that you, too, had just had a broken romance. For myself I realised absolutely within a few days of meeting you again at the hospital that I had fallen for you as I never had for anyone else. It was like a bombshell!'

Was this the old charm again—was he spinning her a yarn? Iona screwed up her eyes against the low evening sun and looked at Matt's handsome, sensitive face. There was no doubt about the torment she could see in his eyes, and how the guilt had lived with him since that awful tragedy. Matt may have taken life lightly before that, but he wasn't a callous, calculating person. She swallowed, gradually realising what a blind fool she'd been, leaping to conclusions and believing that someone as honest as Matt would take up his father's offer to marry someone just for money.

She looked at him for a second, overcome by embarrassment at the insults she'd thrown at him, her words coming back to haunt her.

'Oh, Matt,' she whispered, 'I'm so ashamed. I've been such a stupid idiot…and I'm so sorry. Will you ever forgive me?'

She wound her arms around his neck and pulled down his face to hers, kissing him softly on his mouth.

'There's nothing to forgive,' he said.

'Yes, there is,' she said dolefully, 'I was so censorious about you, when you at least tried to be honest with Shelley. I allowed myself to be swept along with Kevin—too blind to see until the last minute that he wasn't the man for me. I should have examined my feelings more closely and then I wouldn't have humiliated him so much.'

'What made you decide that you couldn't marry him at the last minute, then?' asked Matt curiously. 'Didn't you have any doubts before?'

'He made me feel very special,' Iona explained sadly. 'And after you'd left for Africa, I felt very bereft—I couldn't stop thinking about you. Everyone seemed to be encouraging me to fall for Kevin and because I was lonely I think I persuaded myself that he and I had a future.'

'But to leave it until the actual day…'

'I know. All I can say is that it was better than after the ceremony.'

'But what actually made you realise you'd done the wrong thing?'

'It was my father,' she said simply. 'He made me see the light. Just as we were about to go up the aisle he looked at me very lovingly and said, "Remember darling, this is for the rest of your life—make sure you've got it right like your mother and I did!"'

Matt nodded understandingly at her. 'And that made you realise the gravity of the whole situation, did it?'

'Exactly! His words hit me like a thunderbolt and the commitment I was about to make suddenly seemed completely wrong. When I looked at Kevin, it wasn't his face I saw but yours! I knew I was about to make the most terrible mistake of my life—and Kevin's. I couldn't possibly spend the rest of my life with him!'

Iona shivered and Matt gathered her fiercely in an

embrace that pressed his body so closely to hers that there was no doubt about his passionate desire for her.

'It took some courage to do that, sweetheart,' he said softly. 'And I can understand why you did it. If you had gone ahead, two people—make that three people—would have been very unhappy.'

'But I shall never forgive myself for hurting him so much...I think it will haunt me for ever.'

'Look, Iona, we've got to look to the future now—no good tearing yourself apart when in the end what you did was hard but right,' said Matt firmly, putting his hand under her chin and holding her face towards his. Then he smiled down at her and drew her close to him, his lips fastening on hers with insistent firmness, teasing them apart gently, until she forgot the old guilt and thought only of her longing for him.

He drew away from her for a second, laughing a low, throaty laugh. 'We've got some making up to do, my darling—and won't that be fun?'

Then the sound of an ambulance siren screaming up the drive made them spring apart rather guiltily.

'We'll have the fun later,' he promised, holding her hand as they ran back to the hospital.

EPILOGUE

THERE was a tremendous roar from the engines as the plane took off from the runway and a few second later floated effortlessly in the air. Iona peered out of the window and saw the little villages and roads with toy-like cars on them become smaller and smaller, then disappear gradually beneath the layer of white clouds. Then they were up in the blue sky, hardly moving at all, it seemed.

She took a deep breath and leaned back in her seat, hardly able to believe that a few weeks ago the world had looked so grim—and now, such a short time later, her cup of happiness was full.

It had truly been the most magical day of her life and a kaleidoscope of happy images spun round in her mind.

Matt took her hand and grinned at her. 'How are you, Mrs. Carter?' He leaned over and kissed Iona's neck, sending a thrill of excitement flickering through her. 'And what is my beautiful wife thinking about?'

'I'm thinking what a wonderful day we've had,' she said, smiling at him, her hazel eyes sparkling at him happily. 'The church and the marquee with all our friends and family, and the dancing…but most especially you, Dr Carter, the most handsome man there. And I got you!'

'I rather think it was the other way round,' said Matt, nuzzling into her hair. 'I won the prize. I don't know if I deserve you, but I'm going to do my best to make you happy, my love.'

Tears filled Iona's eyes. 'I couldn't be happier than I am now, Matt. It's been the best day of my life. I don't ever want it to end!'

Matt turned her head to his and looked very tenderly into her eyes. 'It's only just beginning, my darling—only just beginning!'

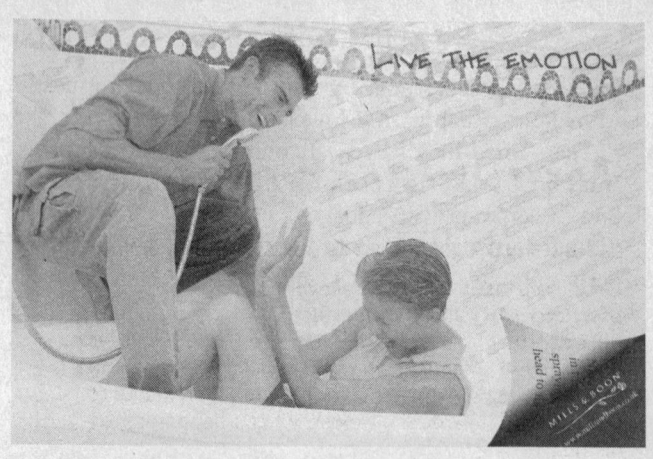

Modern Romance™
...seduction and
passion guaranteed

Tender Romance™
...love affairs that
last a lifetime

Medical Romance™
...medical drama
on the pulse

Historical Romance™
...rich, vivid and
passionate

Sensual Romance™
...sassy, sexy and
seductive

Blaze Romance™
...the temperature's
rising

27 new titles every month.

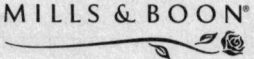

MILLS & BOON®

MB3

the
Mother's Day
collection

Margaret Way   Kate Hoffmann   Helen Dickson

Money Off
Voucher
see inside for details

Available from 21st February 2003

Available at most branches of WH Smith,
Tesco, Martins, Borders, Eason, Sainsbury's
and all good paperback bookshops.

0303/024/MB65

2 BOOKS

AND A SURPRISE GIFT!

We would like to take this opportunity to thank you for reading this Mills & Boon® book by offering you the chance to take TWO more specially selected titles from the Medical Romance™ series absolutely FREE! We're also making this offer to introduce you to the benefits of the Reader Service™—

- ★ FREE home delivery
- ★ FREE monthly Newsletter
- ★ FREE gifts and competitions
- ★ Exclusive Reader Service discount
- ★ Books available before they're in the shops

Accepting these FREE books and gift places you under no obligation to buy; you may cancel at any time, even after receiving your free shipment. Simply complete your details below and return the entire page to the address below. *You don't even need a stamp!*

YES! Please send me 2 free Medical Romance books and a surprise gift. I understand that unless you hear from me, I will receive 4 superb new titles every month for just £2.60 each, postage and packing free. I am under no obligation to purchase any books and may cancel my subscription at any time. The free books and gift will be mine to keep in any case.

M3ZEC

Ms/Mrs/Miss/Mr ....Initials ....
BLOCK CAPITALS PLEASE

Surname ....

Address ....

....

....Postcode ....

Send this whole page to:
UK: FREEPOST CN81, Croydon, CR9 3WZ
EIRE: PO Box 4546, Kilcock, County Kildare (stamp required)